ABSOLUTE CERTAINTY

ROSE CONNORS

SCRIBNER

NEW YORK   LONDON   TORONTO   SYDNEY   SINGAPORE

SCRIBNER
1230 Avenue of the Americas
New York, NY 10020

SCRIBNER and design are trademarks of
Macmillan Library Reference USA, Inc., used under license
by Simon & Schuster, the publisher of this work.

For information about special discounts for bulk purchases,
please contact Simon & Schuster Special Sales:
1-800-456-6798 or business@simonandschuster.com

Designed by Colin Joh
Text set in Sabon

Manufactured in the United States of America

1   3   5   7   9   10   8   6   4   2

Library of Congress Cataloging-in-Publication Data
Connors, Rose
Absolute certainty / Rose Connors
p.   cm.
1. Cape Cod (Mass.)—Fiction. I. Title.
PS3603.O65 A64 2002
813'.6—dc21   2002022915

ISBN 0-7432-2906-1

For Alice and Tom

ACKNOWLEDGMENTS

Precious details in this book were provided by generous friends. To all of them—Garland Alcock, M.D., Bob and Rosemarie Denn, Ron Eppler, and Captain Eddie Reid—heartfelt thanks.

Sincere thanks also to Amy Andreasson, reference librarian extraordinaire, and the amazing staff at the Eldredge.

To Nancy Yost and Susanne Kirk—wow—thank you.

Finally, thanks to my husband, David, for pointing me in the right direction; to my sons, Dave and Sam, for thriving on takeout; and to my sister, Peggy, whose words were an inspiration.

AUTHOR'S NOTE

Many of the fictitious characters who inhabit the pages of this novel bear well-known Cape Cod surnames. This was done solely to add an air of authenticity to the story. No character in these pages is based on any real person, living or dead.

The jury instruction delivered in chapter six, from which this book takes its title, is based on the actual instruction from *Allen versus United States*, 164 U.S. 492, 17 S. Ct. 154 (1896), and is still in use today.

ABSOLUTE CERTAINTY

Three promises. When we selected the jury for *Commonwealth versus Rodriguez,* I asked each prospective juror to make three solemn promises.

First, promise to look slowly and carefully at every exhibit. The blood-soaked windbreaker, tee shirt, and baseball cap. The eight-by-ten close-ups of the fractured skull, sliced throat, and lacerated torso.

Second, promise to listen intently to all of the testimony. The police officer's graphic description of the young man's body at the water's edge. The Medical Examiner's tedious detail about the impact of each knife wound.

And finally, promise to rely on your own gut when you make your decision. Your practical judgment. Your common sense.

We impaneled seven men and five women. All of them promised. And I believe they kept their promises. It was the criminal justice system that failed.

CHAPTER I

Wednesday, May 26

"You nailed him, Martha."

I know it's Geraldine Schilling without looking up. She's the only one in the office—or anywhere else for that matter—who calls me Martha. Geraldine is the First Assistant District Attorney for Barnstable County, a county that includes all the towns on Cape Cod. She intends to be Barnstable County's next District Attorney, a position no woman has ever held.

"You nailed him. Now let's go in there and finish it."

"I'm ready, Geraldine."

I snap my briefcase shut and gesture for Geraldine to take the only empty seat in my cramped office. "But Judge Carroll released the jurors for lunch. He'll call for closing arguments when they get back."

Geraldine doesn't sit down. She never does. She leans against my old wooden file cabinet instead, pressing a spiked heel against the bottom drawer. She draws hard on her cigarette and rolls her pale green eyes to the ceiling. "Lunch? Who the hell eats lunch?"

There is a widely held belief in our office that Geraldine doesn't eat—ever. All of us have seen her attend professional luncheons and political dinners, but no one has seen her swallow a morsel of food. Caffeine and nicotine seem to keep her going. She weighs 110 pounds wearing her neatly tailored suit.

Kevin Kydd appears in my doorway, grinning as usual. "I do. I eat lunch. Where are we going, ladies?"

He always makes me laugh. But Geraldine doesn't crack a smile. She shakes her long blond bangs and blows a steady stream of smoke toward the doorway. "Lunch with you, Kydd? I'd sooner starve."

His grin expands. "Ah, Gerry, you're a peach."

Kevin Kydd arrived in our office one year ago, a young Southern gentleman fresh out of Emory Law School in Atlanta, Georgia. He is tall and lanky, with slightly stooped shoulders and a grin that doesn't quit. Geraldine christened him "the Kydd" immediately upon his arrival and the rest of us adopted it. He, in turn, calls her "Gerry," always with the grin. We marvel that he still has a job.

The Kydd ambles in and settles in the chair Geraldine rejected. "How about you, Marty? My treat."

"Thanks, Kydd, but I'll have to pass. I'm expecting Judge Carroll's clerk to call any time now. We're closing *Rodriguez* this afternoon."

"Mind if I watch?"

The Kydd's question is intended more for Geraldine than for me, but I answer him quickly. "Not a bit."

I remember my early days in this office, handling the traffic offenses and bounced checks that the Kydd is stuck with now, waiting for an opportunity to prosecute a "real" crime. Whenever I could, I watched closing arguments in the more serious cases. I watched

Geraldine in action in a number of trials. She doesn't try cases anymore, but she was excellent in her day.

The old black phone on my desk doesn't finish its first ring before I grab it. "Marty Nickerson."

It's Wanda Morgan, Judge Carroll's courtroom clerk. The jury is back; the judge is calling for summations.

I head for the door. The Kydd reaches it before I do, but he pauses to look back at Geraldine, to verify that he has her permission. She blows a smoke ring at him.

"Go ahead," she says. "Maybe you'll learn something."

CHAPTER 2

In the Commonwealth of Massachusetts, the prosecuting attorney always argues last, just before the judge gives instructions on the law. Having the last word can be a big advantage. I begin speaking to the jurors—quietly—as I walk to the evidence table set up in front of the judge's bench.

"Judge Carroll will instruct you that you should convict this defendant of first-degree murder if you find that he murdered Michael Scott with extreme atrocity or cruelty."

"This defendant" is Manuel Rodriguez, a twenty-six-year-old punk with a rap sheet as long as he is. Throughout this trial, I refused to say his name in front of the jury. I refused to say anything that might suggest he is human. I want them to see him as an animal, an animal unfit to live among the civilized, an animal they should lock away for the rest of its miserable days.

I select two color photographs from the evidence table and pause to stare at Rodriguez. He glares back at me. This is good. I turn my back to him and walk toward the jury box, photos in hand. Some members of the panel avert their eyes; one turns her entire face away. But most, I am pleased to see, look from the bloody scenes to Rodriguez. I hope he is glaring back at them.

"This, people, is extreme atrocity. This is cruelty."

I mean every word of it. I have been an Assistant District Attorney in Barnstable County for more than a decade, handling rapes and homicides for more than half of those years. Stranger homicides like this don't happen here. Crime scenes as grisly as this don't belong here. Killers so utterly void of remorse don't live here.

"Two different witnesses told you they saw this defendant near the Chatham Light just after two in the morning last Memorial Day. Dr. Skinner told you that Michael Scott drew his last breath between two and four o'clock that morning. His lifeless body was found on Lighthouse Beach at daybreak."

Dr. Jeffrey Skinner is a Harvard-educated pathologist who has been Barnstable County's Medical Examiner for almost twenty years. Even he was visibly shaken by the condition of this corpse.

I shift my gaze to the courtroom's front row, where the Scott family sits silently. At my direction, they've sat in that spot all week—Mom, Dad, and two younger brothers. I want the panel to follow my eyes, to look at that diminished family. I want every juror on this panel to remember that the bloody corpse in these gruesome photographs was a son, a big brother, a twenty-year-old college kid with his whole life ahead of him.

I walk back to the evidence table and hold up a third photograph, this one a close-up of the back of Michael's head. His dark matted hair is barely visible through the dried blood.

"Dr. Skinner told you that Michael was hit from behind with an object so heavy it fractured his skull. The contour of the fracture led the doctor to believe the attacker was left-handed."

I turn and point at Rodriguez.

"This defendant is left-handed."

I trade the photograph in for another and carry it to the jury box. It is a view of the bluff in front of Chatham Light.

"Detective Walter Bucknell told you that Michael was dragged through the beach plums, unconscious, down this hill to the sand below. The weight of his body left a trail that was still visible at daybreak. And there were boot prints in the wet sand at the bottom of that trail. Detective Bucknell measured those prints. He stretched his tape measure out beside them and took a picture. Here it is. The tread matches a pair of Viking fish boots, size ten."

Again I point at Rodriguez. "This defendant was arrested at noon that day. He was wearing a pair of Viking fish boots, size ten."

I hold the next photo close to my jacket. "I know how hard this is. But you made a solemn promise to look carefully at all of the evidence. And it is my duty to review it with you."

I turn the picture toward them; almost all of them look away. Their discomfort is palpable. The photo is a close-up of Michael Scott's neck, his throat slit.

"Dr. Skinner told you that Michael had regained consciousness, and was struggling, when the killer slit his throat. In this photograph, you can see the dreadful details."

Minutes pass and still I hold the photo in front of them. I won't put it down until each juror has examined the slice through Michael Scott's throat. This is important. The defense attorney hammered on the only weakness in my case, and I need to respond.

"The defense made much of the fact that the murder weapon was never found. But remember, people, we know a lot about that weapon. We know that Michael Scott was murdered with a blade fine enough and sharp enough to cut like a scalpel. We know that blade was made of high carbon steel, just like the blade of the Dexter Ripper, a knife used on all of our local commercial fishing boats. We also know that this defendant, when he works at all, works as a deckhand on a local lobster boat. We know he had easy access to those knives."

I had wanted to introduce a Dexter Ripper into evidence, but Judge Carroll wouldn't hear of it. The defense attorney had barely gotten to his feet when the judge sustained his objection. On reflection, I believe the judge's ruling was right. And I want him to be right. My gut tells me this jury will convict, and I don't want the conviction reversed on appeal.

I hold up an evidence bag, one of thirty-nine bearing "Commonwealth Exhibit" tags.

"Detective Bucknell told you this flannel shirt was found rolled in a ball in the trunk of this defendant's car. There is blood on the left cuff and the right upper sleeve. Dr. Skinner told you the blood on this shirt is Type AB, same as Michael Scott's. This defendant, the doctor told you, is O positive."

On appeal, the defense will challenge the introduction of Rodriguez's blood type into evidence. The defense bar routinely argues that the use of physical evidence taken from a defendant, such as fingerprints, handwriting, and blood samples, violates the defendant's constitutional privilege against self-incrimination. I am not overly concerned about this issue. The high court has held more than once that the privilege protects only against compulsion of testimony, not against production of real, or physical, evidence.

I turn the evidence bag so they can all see the dark red stains on the plaid shirt.

"DNA testing confirms that this blood—on the defendant's shirt—is Michael Scott's. No one else's." A few of the jurors are nodding. They're with me.

The last photos I intend to use during this argument are two close-ups of Michael's torso. In one, the torso is covered with blood. In the other, taken during the autopsy after the body had been cleaned, the knife wounds are clear.

"It's no wonder there are bloodstains on the shirt, people. As Michael Scott lay on the beach, his throat slit, literally drowning in his own fluids, this defendant sliced him again. He cut Michael open from the middle of his collarbone to his navel, then again from his right hip to his left, and yet again from his right shoulder to his left."

When I first saw the body in the morgue, after it had been cleaned, I was struck by how closely the torso wounds, when viewed from directly above, looked like a capital *I,* or maybe a Roman numeral I. The image isn't as clear from these photos, though, and it's not a point I raised with the jury. I look at the photographs myself, then hold them up for the panel.

"Remember Dr. Skinner's testimony, people. Michael Scott didn't have time to drown. He bled to death first."

Mrs. Scott's sobs fill the courtroom. I am truly sorry for her pain—after all, I'm a mother too—but I am also acutely aware that her timing is perfect. Her breakdown has a visible impact on the jurors. I'm not surprised when the defense requests a break in the proceedings.

Judge Carroll announces a fifteen-minute recess, during which it is understood that I will gently advise Sally Scott she must either compose herself or leave the courtroom. I know how badly she wants to stay to the end. It's all she can do for her firstborn son now.

CHAPTER 3

Charlie Cahoon has been a bailiff in the Barnstable County Superior Court for thirty-five years. He has seen more trials than most lawyers. He has earned the complete confidence of the judges who preside here. And he is one of my favorite people.

I went all through the Chatham school system with Charlie's son, Jake. During my second year of law school I came back to Cape Cod just once, for Jake's wedding. Jake married his high school sweetheart, one of my best childhood friends, and a year later Jake Junior was born. Jake Junior had just celebrated his first birthday when his parents were killed in a car accident on the Mid-Cape Highway.

Charlie was already a widower when his only son and daughter-in-law died, and he has raised his grandson all by himself. Jake Junior is eighteen now, a popular high school senior and a star basketball player. He has a heart of gold, just like his grandfather. My son, Luke, a high school junior, idolizes him.

Charlie is in charge of the jurors. He leads them in and out of the courtroom each day. He arranges their lunches. And in a case like this one, where the jurors will be sequestered once they begin deliberations, Charlie will arrange their dinners and hotel accommodations as well.

When Charlie leads the jurors into the courtroom after the break, most of them send sympathetic glances to the now composed Sally Scott. Not one of them looks at Rodriguez. This bodes poorly for him. Human beings don't like to make eye contact with a man they think butchered a fellow human being.

I stand in front of the jury box and hold up another evidence bag. "This is Michael Scott's watch. Michael's dad told you that he and his wife gave it to Michael when he graduated from high school. They had his initials—MVS—engraved on the wristband."

I have planned this moment carefully. I turn my back to the jurors, walk to the opposite side of the courtroom, and stand still in front of the defense table. I stare at Rodriguez in silence for a minute before I face the jury again. I point squarely at him. My finger is barely a foot from his face.

"This defendant had Michael Scott's watch. It was crammed into the front left pocket of his jeans. Detective Bucknell told you that, people. Remember his testimony. He told you this defendant had Michael's watch and he told you this defendant had Michael's tips— seventy-two dollars and fifty cents."

I retrieve another evidence bag, this one stuffed with bills—mostly singles—and a fistful of change. Michael Scott had only recently arrived on Cape Cod to work for the summer. He'd planned to return to Boston University for his junior year at the end of the season. He found work waiting tables at the Chatham Pearl, an upscale pub serving a wealthy clientele during the summer months. The season had barely begun when Michael Scott was murdered. His body was found during the early morning hours on Memorial Day, almost a year ago.

"Of course we can't prove beyond all doubt that these dollars and coins are Michael's tips. After all, no one marked his money. But remember, people, each of you made a solemn promise to call on your common sense—your gut—when you looked at this evidence. Now it's time to keep that promise."

I move so close to Rodriguez I can hear him breathing and, for the first time since I left my chair, I raise my voice.

"Listen to your gut when you look at these facts, people. Michael left the Pearl shortly after his shift ended at two A.M. When his body was found just hours later, his pockets were empty and his watch was gone. When this defendant was picked up at noon, his pockets were full and Michael's watch was still ticking. Common sense, people. This defendant murdered Michael Scott and went home with seventy-two dollars, fifty cents, and a wristwatch."

I pause here and walk slowly back to the jury box, deliberately making eye contact with every juror. Each one returns my look with a level gaze. This is good. Jurors who look the prosecutor in the eye at the end of a case are generally inclined to convict. I lower my voice again.

"The defense attorney would like you to believe that this defendant is guilty only of theft from a corpse. Revolting, perhaps, but certainly not first-degree murder. The defense has argued that some depraved third party must have killed Michael Scott; that Michael was already dead when this defendant happened upon him; that this defendant did nothing more than help himself to the spoils."

The defense attorney is Harry Madigan, a man I know well and admire. He was two classes ahead of me in law school, and he has been with the Barnstable County Public Defender's office his entire career. He is a worthy opponent, always thoroughly prepared and quick on his feet. Harry routinely gives each client a better defense than most highly paid attorneys in private practice could muster. He didn't have much to work with this time. Given Rodriguez's lengthy record, Harry couldn't even put his client on the witness stand.

I raise my voice again.

"But this defendant's argument doesn't work, people. It doesn't work because it defies our common sense. Look at the evidence. Michael Scott's killer was left-handed; this defendant is left-handed. Michael Scott's killer was wearing Viking fish boots, size ten; this defendant—arrested just hours after the murder—was wearing Viking fish boots, size ten. Michael Scott's throat was slit with a fine blade made of high-carbon steel, just like the blade of a Dexter Ripper; this defendant had access to those knives any day he showed up for work. Michael's blood was on this defendant's shirt, a shirt he rolled into a ball and hid in the trunk of his car. Michael's tips and wristwatch were in his pockets."

I lean on the railing of the jury box and look at each of them. I lower my voice yet again to just above a whisper. I am pleased when three jurors in the back row lean forward to listen.

"Common sense, people. When Judge Carroll gives you his instructions, he will tell you that you are not to leave your good judgment outside the courtroom door. He will tell you that your good judgment is one of the main reasons you were chosen to sit on this jury. He will tell you that we're all counting on you to use that good judgment now.

"I never met Michael Scott, people. And I never will. You will never meet him either. And yet it is your job to speak for him. By your verdict, you must do for him what he can no longer do for himself. Speak.

"The word *verdict* comes from the Latin—*veritas dictum,* which means 'speak the truth.' Do it, people. Speak the truth."

CHAPTER 4

Friday, May 28

"What the hell do they need, a videotape of the crime in progress? What's taking so long?"

Geraldine has been in and out of my office all morning. Now she's followed me into the lunchroom. The jury has been out almost two full days—longer than any of us had expected—and Geraldine is a wreck. The rule of thumb among criminal law practitioners is that the longer a jury is out, the less likely it is to convict.

I pour a cup of coffee and sink into the nearest old wooden chair. "Relax, Geraldine. We gave them a lot of evidence. It took a week. These are conscientious jurors; they'll look at all of it before they come back."

Telling Geraldine to relax is like telling a pit bull to act like a golden retriever. The truth is, though, I am anything but relaxed myself. Few creatures on the planet are so tortured as the lawyer awaiting a verdict after a murder trial, and I am no exception. Helpless to do anything further for the Scott family, I've been equally unable to focus on any other task since Wednesday.

The waiting is not made any easier, of course, by Geraldine's constant hounding. She flicks her cigarette ashes into the sink and focuses those green eyes of hers on the wall clock. "Conscientious jurors, huh? We'll see how damned conscientious they are in a couple of hours."

Geraldine is referring to a phenomenon well documented by trial attorneys throughout the country. Deliberating jurors, even those who appear sharply divided, have a remarkable ability to resolve their differences when Friday afternoon rolls around. Cape Cod attorneys take this maxim one step further. The verdict will be in by three o'clock, they say, if it's Friday before a summer holiday weekend.

It's one o'clock on Friday before Memorial Day. Geraldine expects this verdict within two hours.

I loathe the idea of jurors compromising their convictions to safeguard the leisure of a long weekend, but I won't argue about it with Geraldine. I learned years ago that her jaded view of the jury system is not something I can fix. I'm spared the need to respond when the Kydd leans into the lunchroom.

"Marty, Wanda called. The jury is ready to come back, but not with a verdict. They've sent word with Charlie that they're hopelessly deadlocked."

CHAPTER 5

Our offices are on the first floor of the District Courthouse. I head out as soon as the Kydd delivers his message, though I know that means I'll arrive in the Superior Courtroom too soon. Harry Madigan's office is ten minutes away, and Judge Carroll doesn't take the bench for any hearing until both sides are present. The truth is I look forward to the short wait. I love being in the Superior Courtroom alone.

The Barnstable County Complex consists of four buildings arranged rectangularly. The Probate Court and the District Court make up the short sides of the rectangle. One of the long sides is bordered by a tall chain-link fence topped with electrified barbed wire, beyond which looms the redbrick Barnstable County House of Correction. There are more than a few residents of that facility who would give their right arms for five minutes alone with me.

Directly across from the jail is the back entrance to the Superior Courthouse, but I spend the extra couple of minutes to walk in the sunshine out to Main Street in Barnstable Village. I approach the courthouse from the front, and the view is impressive. It's an imposing Greek Revival structure, almost two hundred years old, listed on the National Register of Historic Places. The original gray granite building has undergone five major alterations since its construction, but it still has only one courtroom. The rest of the building is devoted to office space, meeting rooms, and document storage.

Two large cannons rest on the front lawn of the Superior Courthouse. They were dragged here from Boston by oxen after the War of 1812. Behind the cannons, four grand pillars frame the imposing front entrance. Few people realize that the pillars, though massive and solid-looking, are actually hollow.

The solitary courtroom is on the second floor, and it's empty when I arrive, just as expected. It's not a very large room, but it is stately. The judge's bench, jury box, witness stand, counsel tables, and spectator pews are all made of highly polished mahogany. Behind the raised judge's bench are floor-to-ceiling bookcases, also mahogany, lined with hardbound volumes of Massachusetts case law. Behind the jury box hangs a large pendulum clock in a glass case. Framed portraits of retired judges—most of them bearded—line the walls.

The lower half of every wall is covered with mahogany wainscoting; the upper half is painted a deep ivory. Each sidewall contains six rectangular windows which extend to the full height of the two-story room, admitting a flood of natural light through sheer, cream-colored curtains. Additional light is provided by four elaborate chandeliers. The thick wall-to-wall carpeting weaves ivory, maroon, and hunter green hues in a floral design.

In the back of the room there is a small loft for those rare cases, like this one, which draw overflow crowds. Behind the mahogany dowels of the loft's banister are two elongated deacon's benches for additional seating.

During the courtroom's most recent renovation, a suspended ceiling was removed, and the room's original dome was revealed and preserved. A circular plaster frieze in the center of the ceiling was restored. Delicate stenciling around the perimeter of the frieze was enhanced. And there, suspended from the middle of the frieze, from the pinnacle of the room, was a large tin codfish—the official symbol of the Commonwealth of Massachusetts. The codfish was refurbished in painstaking detail, then returned to its prominent spot overlooking all of the proceedings in Superior Court.

At times like this, when I am alone in here, I remember why I chose this profession, why I turned my back on higher-paying jobs with private law firms. Even now, after more than a decade of prosecuting, I believe in what I do. I am proud to represent the Commonwealth against thugs like Rodriguez. I am eager to serve as a surrogate for those whose voices have been wrongly silenced. I am honored to champion the causes of families like the Scotts.

The Scotts surprise me when they walk through the courtroom's back door. They would have been notified, of course, if the jury were returning with a final decision. But a jury's initial report that it's deadlocked is almost never treated as final, particularly when Judge Herbert Carroll presides. Wanda would not have summoned them from their hotel for this hearing. They must be spending their days in the courthouse hallway, waiting.

They move toward me as a group, as if the physical proximity to one another is all that holds each of them upright. I see by their alarmed expressions that someone—probably Charlie—told them the jury is deadlocked.

The middle Scott boy—now the oldest, I realize as they walk toward me—is sixteen, same as my son, Luke. I've grown to admire this young man during the course of the trial. He is protective toward his parents and younger brother, concerned with their grief as they relive the nightmare, somehow managing his own. I'm not surprised when he is the first of them to speak.

"Do they think that creep didn't do it? Are they saying he didn't do all that to Mike?"

His raspy voice is angry and the tears in his eyes are about to spill over. In another setting, I would hug him. Instead, I pat his arm and direct my comments to all of them.

"No, that's not what they're saying. They're telling us they're worried that they won't be able to agree on a verdict. Some of them think he's guilty and some of them—we don't know how many—aren't sure."

Mr. Scott finds his voice. "So what happens now?"

"Legal argument," I tell him. "I'll ask the judge to instruct the jury to go back and try again. Attorney Madigan will argue that this is a hung jury, that the judge should declare a mistrial and send the jurors home."

The Scotts nod at me and move silently into their regular front row spot. They are numb.

I could spare them this anxiety. I could tell them—truthfully—that the legal argument they are about to hear is a mere formality, a technical device employed only to allow the defense lawyer to preserve this issue for appeal. I could tell them that Harry Madigan and I both know he will lose this argument, that Judge Carroll always gives the "go back and try again" instruction. I could tell them that the instruction Judge Carroll will give is known as the "dynamite charge" among members of the bar because it almost always jolts a stagnant jury into reaching a verdict.

I could tell them all of that—just as I could have told dozens of nervous families before them—but I won't. I won't for the same reasons a devoted daughter won't divulge her family's secrets to the neighbors.

The criminal justice system shouldn't work this way. Reasonable doubt is a slippery concept. Some part of me has always agreed with Harry Madigan's contention that a deadlocked jury is reasonable doubt personified. At the very least, Harry's argument should be analyzed and considered seriously.

But Judge Carroll is sixty-eight years old, just two years away from mandatory retirement. He has been on the bench for twenty-two years. He is weary. He is kind and patient with witnesses and jurors, but just plain tired of lawyers and arguments.

Harry rushes in and remains standing—tapping one foot—in front of the defense table. I like everything about Harry, but the thing I like best is his persistence. Through every case—through every argument, even—Harry nurtures an eternal, stubborn hope that Judge Carroll will actually listen to him.

The judge takes the bench and adjusts his glasses before he looks down at us. His eyes say, "I've heard it all before."

CHAPTER 6

Harry isn't actually shouting at Judge Carroll as he wraps up his argument, but he's dangerously close.

"This trial is over, Judge. These jurors can't agree, and they have an absolute right to disagree. What we have here is reasonable doubt, Judge, plain and simple. This court should declare a mistrial and send them all home."

Judge Carroll barely looks up from his bench. "Thank you, Mr. Madigan. Ms. Nickerson?"

"Your Honor, my Brother is correct in saying that the jurors have a right to disagree. They do. But the Supreme Judicial Court has held in dozens of cases that giving the dynamite charge doesn't deprive them of that right."

I cite all the pertinent decisions, knowing very well that Judge Carroll is signing orders in other cases as I speak. When I finish, it takes a full minute for him to realize I've stopped talking. He looks up abruptly, startled by the silence, and a lock of thin gray hair falls over the left lens of his frameless bifocals.

"Thank you, Ms. Nickerson. And you as well, Mr. Madigan. The court thanks both attorneys for their presentations. Now, having considered the arguments, I intend to give these jurors my standard dynamite charge. You've both seen it before. Mr. Madigan, should the court reporter note your usual objections?"

"Yes, Judge," Harry sighs.

Judge Carroll nods to the stenographer, who has all of Harry's objections to this instruction on record. The Court of Appeals has upheld Judge Carroll's dynamite charge over Harry's objections in a half-dozen cases. The judge nods again, this time to Charlie, who hurries out the side door and returns moments later with the jurors.

The holdouts are easily identified. Juror number six, a retired English teacher, and juror number ten, a young hairstylist, are both in tears. Both women stare at the floor with swollen eyes and red faces, their makeup smudged. A few of the men look furious. And every one of these jurors wears the tortured expression of turmoil.

Harry is craning forward over the defense table, trying to make eye contact with the two holdouts, hoping to give them a nod of encouragement, I presume. But neither woman so much as lifts her sore eyes from the floor.

Judge Carroll, speaking slowly and deliberately, gives them the dynamite:

"Ladies and gentlemen of the jury. In a large number of cases, and perhaps strictly speaking in all cases, absolute certainty cannot be attained, nor can it be expected. The verdict to which a juror agrees must, of course, be his or her own verdict, the result of his or her own convictions, and not a mere acquiescence in the conclusions of fellow jurors. Yet, in order to bring twelve minds to a unanimous result, you must examine the questions submitted to you with candor, and with the proper regard and deference to the opinions of each other."

One of the men in front turns completely around in his chair to stare accusingly at the red-eyed hairdresser. Apparently, he doesn't feel the young woman showed the proper regard and deference toward his opinion.

"You should consider that you are selected in the same manner and from the same pool as any future jury must be selected. There is no reason to suppose that this case will ever be submitted to twelve men and women more intelligent, more impartial, or more competent to decide it. There is also no reason to suppose that more or clearer evidence will be produced on one side or the other. With these considerations in mind, it is your duty to decide the case, if you can do so without violence to your individual judgment."

Harry wheels his chair around to face the panel. He does this every time. It's his way of adding emphasis to the judge's last phrase. And it's the first of many silent messages Harry will attempt to send to the jury during the dynamite charge.

Harry's little one-man show has never had an impact on any jury, as far as I can tell. But it always annoys Judge Carroll. The judge pauses just long enough to fire a cautionary stare in Harry's direction. Harry ignores him. The judge continues.

"In the event you cannot so decide, a jury has a right to fail to agree. In order to make a decision more practical, the law imposes a burden of proof on one party or the other in all cases. The high burden of proof which must be sustained by the prosecution has not changed. In this case the burden of proof is on the Commonwealth to establish each and every element of the offense beyond a reasonable doubt. And if with respect to any single element you are left in reasonable doubt, the defendant is entitled to the benefit of that doubt and must be acquitted."

Harry is nodding now, his elbows on the table, his chin on his hands. This judge is a wise man, his expression telegraphs. We should all listen to him.

"But in conferring together you ought to pay proper respect to each other's opinions and you ought to listen with a disposition to being convinced of each other's arguments. When there is disagreement, each juror favoring acquittal should consider whether a doubt in his or her own mind is a reasonable one when it makes no impression upon the minds of the other equally honest and equally intelligent jurors."

Harry scowls at the panel now. No juror favoring acquittal should do any such thing.

"All of you heard the same evidence and gave it the same degree of attention. All of you are deliberating under sanction of the same oath. All of you are charged with the same duty to arrive at the truth.

"On the other hand, jurors favoring conviction ought seriously to ask themselves whether they should doubt the correctness of a judgment which is not concurred in by others on this panel. Reexamine the weight and sufficiency of that evidence which fails to carry conviction in the minds of your fellow jurors."

The judge is wise again. Harry is nodding once more.

"Finally, not only should jurors in the minority reexamine their positions, but jurors in the majority should do so as well. Ask yourselves whether you have given careful consideration to, and placed sufficient weight upon, that evidence which favorably impresses the persons who disagree with you.

"I am instructing you now to go back and resume your deliberations."

With that, Judge Carroll removes his bifocals and nods to Charlie.

Charlie leads the silent jurors out the side door. They are resigned. Resigned to spending Memorial Day weekend sequestered. Resigned to observing the holiday with virtual strangers instead of family and friends. Resigned to reexamining their positions, even those who have drawn clear lines in the sand.

I am resigned too. My son is spending this weekend in Boston with his father, and I am resigned to a long weekend of waiting—alone.

CHAPTER 7

My ex-husband is Ralph Ellis, a well-known forensic psychiatrist. He is retained as an expert witness by criminal defendants in cases where their sanity—or lack thereof—is an issue. His offices are on the third floor of a trendy renovated warehouse on Boston Harbor, but he travels all over the country to testify. In the past decade he has appeared in at least a dozen highly publicized trials on behalf of Hollywood celebrities, rock stars, and professional athletes. Only the wealthiest of criminal defendants can afford him.

Ralph and I met when he guest lectured at a forensic evidence seminar during the first semester of my third year at Yale Law School. I was swept off my feet. He was the most brilliant man I'd ever met. And he still is.

We married on the Saturday after I graduated. When our son, Luke, was born thirteen months later, we called ourselves the luckiest—and happiest—people on earth. Ralph brought Luke and me home from the hospital in a brand new Thunderbird convertible—baby blue.

On Luke's sixth birthday, Ralph left. He married his receptionist, a glamorous young thing called Holly, as soon as our divorce was final. It was then that Luke and I moved from Boston to Chatham, the town where I was born and raised. And we took the Thunderbird with us.

Cape Cod is an arm-shaped peninsula and the town of Chatham is its elbow. Luke says living in Chatham is a lot like living on a ship. The town is surrounded on three sides by the salty waters of Nantucket Sound and the Atlantic Ocean. Its year-round population of six thousand enjoys more than eighty miles of breathtaking coastline. With the exception of the summer months, Chatham is quiet.

Until last Memorial Day, random violence was unheard of in Chatham. It's fair to say that the town's innocence died along with Michael Scott last year. My neighbors lock their doors now.

In the decade that followed our return to Chatham, Ralph largely ignored Luke. He made his child support payments on time, and sent an expensive present each Christmas, but otherwise seemed to forget he had a son. That has changed during the past year, though. Ralph and Holly are in the midst of a bitter divorce, and Ralph has been trying to forge a relationship with his only child. It hasn't been easy.

Luke has always been furious with his father for leaving us. After our move to Chatham, he refused to come to the telephone on the rare occasions when Ralph called. When Luke started school, he told his teacher he didn't have a father and didn't think he'd ever had one. Even now, he is curt and short-tempered with Ralph, traits I never see in him with anyone else.

It takes forty-five minutes to drive the old Thunderbird the thirty miles from my office in Barnstable to my home in Chatham. The holiday traffic has arrived. Ralph is pacing in the kitchen when I get home.

"For Christ's sake, Marty, where've you been?"

I'm wearing a gray suit and carrying a briefcase. I wonder where he thinks I've been. "Out dancing," I answer.

"Very funny."

Ralph is annoyed, standing still now. "I get here. It's seven o'clock. You're nowhere to be found. And Luke isn't even packed."

"You were supposed to be here at six," I remind him.

"Marty, he wasn't even packed by seven." Ralph raises his hands to the heavens to show me how exasperated he is.

Luke appears in the kitchen with Danny Boy, our nine-year-old Irish setter, on his heels. Danny Boy stops short when he sees Ralph. His ears stiffen and he growls. I had never heard Danny Boy growl at anyone—not even a stranger—before Ralph started coming to the house. He's been coming here almost every week for about a year now, and Danny Boy growls at him every time. I have to admit—it makes me laugh.

Luke is wearing the expression of a convicted felon at sentencing. He is dreading this weekend with his father. "I'm packed. I'm packed. Geez, I'm only going for two nights."

"Three," I correct him. But he shakes his head.

"Dad has to work Monday. I'm coming back Sunday night."

I turn to Ralph, who has managed to calm down a bit, and is keeping a wary eye on Danny Boy. "You have to work on Memorial Day?"

"I'm flying out of Logan first thing in the morning. I'm scheduled to testify in Seattle on Tuesday."

Seattle. The prosecutors in the infamous Dr. Wu trial rested their case this afternoon. It was all over the radio news on the drive home. The defense must be opening with Ralph. Not a bad strategy.

The self-proclaimed "Doctor" Wu is a Chinese herbalist accused of murdering five of his female patients. The first victim was found with a metal spike through her heart. The second was bludgeoned with a wooden beam, and the third was drowned in a shallow pond. The fourth woman was burned beyond recognition. The fifth was buried alive.

Turns out that Dr. Wu is neither a doctor nor a Wu. His real name is Willie Chung. The word *wu* means "five" in Mandarin, and the Chinese character represents the five elements of herbal medicine: metal, wood, water, fire, and earth.

According to the press, Ralph's psychoanalysis of the good doctor reveals that he suffers from "DID"—Dissociative Identity Disorder— a condition mere mortals might call a split personality. Willie Chung doesn't know anything about these murdered women. But Dr. Wu does.

It takes some effort to resist the urge to cross-examine Ralph, but I manage. Instead, I hug Luke. "See you Sunday night, then. Maybe we'll hit the beach on Monday."

Luke is tall and angular like his father, but he has my fair skin, black hair, and dark blue eyes. At six feet one, he is a good seven inches taller than I am. He has to stoop to return my hug. "Bye, Mom" is all he says.

They are out the kitchen door. I stand on the back deck with Danny Boy and wave until the taillights of Ralph's BMW are out of sight. Luke doesn't realize that I dread this weekend more than he does. The house is far too quiet.

CHAPTER 8

Sunday, May 30

The Kydd is an American history buff, a fact that drives Geraldine crazy. "With all that useless information crammed into your brain," she routinely berates him, "how much space is left for the law?" The Kydd never answers. He usually grins, recites another obscure fact, and waits patiently for her to lambaste him again.

Because he's a first-year lawyer—a neophyte, Geraldine calls him—the Kydd's cases are not the kind that require weekend attention. He has been here both days, though, cleaning out his single file cabinet, archiving closed matters, and stopping by my office every hour or so to share some little-known detail about the Civil War or the First Continental Congress. I appreciate the moral support. I also know he is eager to be here when the jury comes back. We're not likely to see another case like this one in Barnstable County for a long time.

Typically, sequestered jurors are brought from their hotel to the courthouse to deliberate each day from nine to five. These jurors, though, have requested longer hours and Judge Carroll has allowed it. They arrived here at eight on Saturday morning and did not retire until twelve hours later. They were back promptly at eight this morning and now, ten hours into it, they ask Charlie to have dinner delivered to the jury room again so they can continue working.

The Kydd is back in my doorway. "Marty, let's go to Jeff's. They can call us there if anything breaks."

Every year Jeff Skinner throws an elaborate Memorial Day weekend barbecue. He's a superb host. Jeff is a highly decorated veteran who served two tours of duty in the Marine Corps during the Vietnam War before he went to medical school. Maybe that's why he spares no expense on his Memorial Day feast. In addition to the usual hot dogs, hamburgers, and watermelon, Jeff always serves great appetizers from the Cape's best restaurants. He lives on Morris Island, an island that is part of the town of Chatham, connected to the mainland by a mile-long dike.

The Kydd is right; we may as well go. I'm tired of staring at my office walls. Besides, Luke will be home by now, and we can pick him up on the way. Jeff lives just up the road from Rob Mendell, Barnstable County's incumbent District Attorney, and Rob's younger son, Justin, is Luke's best friend. Each boy will go willingly to Jeff's barbecue—or to any office gathering, for that matter—only because he expects the other one to be there.

The traffic is awful—no surprise the night before Memorial Day. The Kydd and I caravan to the small cottage he rents in Brewster, so he can abandon his car in the driveway and ride the rest of the way with me. A full hour after leaving the courthouse, we reach Chatham Center, where the streets and the restaurants are jammed. We continue eastbound, toward Coast Guard Station Chatham and Chatham Light, whose beacon failed to rescue Michael Scott a year ago.

The Kydd, of course, knows a bit of history about this place.

Pointing offshore, where I see nothing but whitecaps, he seems to recognize a particular spot in the waves. "At sunrise on June 20, 1782," he lectures, "crew members from a British privateer were discovered here, in Chatham's East Harbor, trying to steal three unmanned vessels. They wanted them as prizes of war."

The Kydd always assumes a professorial tone when he shares historical trivia.

"The alarm cannon alerted the town militia, which gathered on the beach quickly and opened fire. Their efforts drove the largest of the three coveted vessels aground, and soon thereafter the British gave up. They boarded small boats and hightailed it back to their own ship, anchored offshore. The Chatham militia gave chase in a fleet of small privately owned boats. The would-be thieves escaped, but the Chatham vessels were recovered. The incident became known as the Battle of Chatham Harbor, Chatham's only active participation in the Revolutionary War."

The Kydd tears his eyes from the surf and looks at me silently, a professor awaiting his student's evaluation. "Thank your lucky stars," I tell him, "that Geraldine isn't here."

"But you live here," he protests. "You should know these things." I roll my eyes at him.

After passing Chatham Light, we bear left on Morris Island Road, a road that seems to lead to the end of the earth. Just before land disappears, Morris Island Road turns right. We turn left instead, onto Windmill Lane, where Luke, Danny Boy, and I share a small shingled cottage left to me by my parents. Their only valuable asset, they used to say, besides me. It sits just a few yards from the ocean at high tide.

If we had turned right with Morris Island Road, it would have led us to the dike, or the causeway, as it's called by the locals. After picking up Luke, we head back in that direction. As usual, the causeway is alive with the sounds of seals and shorebirds. The marsh on either side of the two-lane road is teeming with snowy egrets, Canada geese, and long-legged great blue herons.

Morris Island is home to part of the Monomoy National Wildlife Refuge, a jewel of the National Wildlife Refuge System. Designated a Wilderness Area in 1970, it is 2,750 acres of federally protected raw beauty.

Most of the Monomoy Refuge is on North and South Monomoy Islands, two islands south of Morris Island, both accessible only by boat. But forty acres of it are here, on Morris Island, and Luke knows every inch of these forty acres—every sand dune, mudflat, and salt-water marsh—by heart. This refuge is famous for its shorebird migrations and, thanks to Luke, I can identify most of the species that come and go throughout the year. Two endangered species, the piping plover and roseate tern, nest here during the spring and summer. During the fall and winter, the refuge is home to thousands of eiders, scoters, and red-breasted mergansers. Hundreds of harbor seals spend the winter here.

All year long, in all sorts of weather, we walk these beaches. Luke never comes home without a story. He almost always spies red-tailed hawks perched on the treetops. Every spring, he watches through binoculars as osprey pairs feed their young in nests built atop man-made elevated platforms. On rare occasions, he spots a bald eagle or two soaring overhead. Once, he saw a gray seal give birth to pups on the sandy beach.

Jeff Skinner's house is the second one from the refuge. Only Rob Mendell's house is closer. Morris Island Road turns into Tisquantum Road when we leave the dike. We pass the refuge entrance and Rob's cobblestone driveway before climbing the small hill and parking the Thunderbird where dozens of familiar cars are already parked, on the road in front of Jeff's gated estate.

The Town of Chatham is an affluent one—its dump plays Chopin on Sunday afternoons—but Morris Island is especially so. Those who own homes here also own the island itself—the Quitnesset Association, they call themselves. The homes of the Quitnesset Association are old mansions and their owners come from old money, Jeff and Rob included. Jeff's enormous home sits high on a bluff, with perfectly manicured grounds and sweeping views of the Atlantic from every room.

Jeff divorced a while back, and his grown kids live off-Cape somewhere near his ex-wife. He doesn't talk about them much. He's a quiet man, a voracious reader, and an accomplished pianist in addition to being a fine pathologist. I know he's probably as eager as I am to hear the jury's verdict. He saw what Rodriguez did to Michael Scott.

Jeff hurries toward the Kydd and me as soon as we reach his oceanside patio. "Any news?"

I shake my head. "Nothing."

"They're still working, though," the Kydd adds. "They must be making progress."

Jeff signals to a waiter, who hurries toward us with a tray of drinks. "Progress? They should have convicted inside of an hour."

"They'll convict," I tell him. "I have a good feeling about this panel."

Jeff arches his eyebrows at me. I don't usually make predictions.

Soon after we arrive, the glorious May evening begins to surrender to a thick cold mist rolling in from the Atlantic. "Chatham fog" we call it, a frequent summer visitor. Most of Jeff's guests move inside, and soon the fire in the huge stone fireplace is beginning to crackle.

The living room is impressive. It's two stories high and elegantly furnished, Jeff's baby grand piano its focal point, built-in bookcases on every wall. The room is filled with an assortment of people from my office, Jeff's lab, and the courthouse. Even Charlie Cahoon's grandson is here, I'm glad to see, planted in front of the food table with Luke and Justin. He's taller than they are, thinner, too. "Hey, it's my lawyer," he says, pointing his fork at me.

Jake Junior has been calling me his lawyer since he got his driver's license. Just in case, he says. The fact that I'm a prosecutor doesn't seem to bother him.

"What have you done?"

"Nothing yet." He grabs another hot dog. "But I'm young. I've got time." Jake Junior has a small gap between his two front teeth and a dimple on his chin. His lopsided smile always makes me laugh.

"I'm still waiting for that retainer," I tell him.

He winks at me, as if we both know the check's in the mail.

The Kydd and I find Geraldine and Rob Mendell, the man whose job she wants, by the fire. Luke, Justin, and Jake Junior inhale a few hot dogs each, fill paper plates with desserts, and head out to shoot hoops at Rob's house. The Kydd begins a little-known anecdote about the Boston Tea Party, strictly to annoy Geraldine. She launches into her usual tirade which, oddly enough, he seems to enjoy. Rob and I move away from them and watch through the street-side window as the three boys dribble down the slope toward Rob's house, in and out of the fog.

Luke and Justin played varsity basketball this year after spending two years on the junior varsity squad. Jake Junior, who is a class ahead, took them under his wing, becoming a mentor of sorts. Lucky for them. Jake Junior is a basketball legend in Chatham. He's just been awarded a full scholarship to play for Duke University next year. Jake Junior had planned to join the army to finance his college education—his grandfather doesn't earn enough as a court bailiff to pay the tuition at Duke—but that won't be necessary now.

Jake Junior saw to it that Justin and Luke were assigned team shirts with their chosen numbers: Justin's three; Luke's four. The numbers honor their back-to-back birthdays, Justin's on July third and Luke's on July fourth. A couple of firecrackers, I call them.

Rob Mendell was divorced from Justin's mother before I met him. He has an older son, the product of his first marriage, who lives somewhere in California and visits rarely. Rob is a devoted father to Justin—like me, he never misses a basketball game—but I've never learned how he came to have sole custody of his younger son. Luke says he and Justin have an unspoken understanding: Justin doesn't talk about his mother and Luke doesn't talk about his father. Someday, for Luke at least, I hope that will change.

The three tall boys and their plates full of brownies and cupcakes disappear completely in the fog. Rob and I laugh about our growing boys and our mounting grocery bills and, for just a little while, I actually forget about the Rodriguez jury. That's how charming Rob Mendell is.

The phone rings. Jeff answers and finds my eyes through the crowd. The room falls silent.

"You're needed at the courthouse."

CHAPTER 9

Judge Carroll and Harry both look terrible. I probably don't look so hot myself. The judge has elected to hear Harry's motion in chambers, sparing himself the need to don his robe and ascend to his bench at this late hour. Harry wants the judge to excuse the jury for the evening. The stenographer is present to record the argument and its outcome.

Harry skips the formalities. "Judge, if this jury doesn't retire for the night, at least some jurors are going to feel real pressure to compromise their views—to just plain cave in to the others—out of sheer desire to bring an end to the day. They've already been in there too long."

I don't necessarily disagree with Harry, but Judge Carroll doesn't even look in my direction. He leans backward in his leather chair and shakes his head. "Harry, your concern is misplaced. These people want to keep working. They told Charlie they're making progress, and I'm sure as hell not going to stop them. You go on home and get some shut-eye, and we'll call you if there's any news."

Judge Carroll and I both know that Harry isn't going anywhere. And there's not going to be much shut-eye for any of us. Harry is angry, and I don't blame him. This is the kind of decision a trial judge makes that is never reversed on appeal. The appellate courts have no interest in micromanaging jury deliberations. The defendant either wins this argument at the trial level, or he loses it for good.

Harry sets up camp in the darkened courtroom. He renews his motion at eleven-thirty and again at twelve forty-five. He shakes me awake at two o'clock and does it all over again. Judge Carroll grows paler through the early morning hours, but he refuses to budge. Charlie is checking on the jurors at regular intervals, he tells us, and they want to keep working.

At four in the morning, Harry is on his feet and headed toward chambers to continue his crusade. But Judge Carroll emerges in his robe, both hands raised to silence him.

"They're done," he says. "We've got a verdict."

CHAPTER 10

Monday, May 31

Geraldine is the first to arrive, just before five. The Scott family is minutes behind her, hounded by the press. Reporters' questions and photographers' flashbulbs engulf them. One boor from the *Boston Herald* asks how they feel about the verdict being returned on Memorial Day, the anniversary of their son's death. I would like to have him locked up.

The Rodriguez family arrives next. His petite wife and her mother, with two small, curly-haired boys in tow. The boys grow animated when their father is ushered through the side door. They wave to him as if it were a happy coincidence that he is here too.

Like all accused who are imprisoned while on trial, Rodriguez has been issued normal street clothes, minus the belt and shoelaces, to wear in the jury's presence. His cuffs and shackles are removed before the jury is led in. Extra court officers have been summoned to handle him when the verdict is read. Four of them stand behind his chair, guns on their hips, ready to subdue him if necessary.

Rob Mendell barely makes it to his seat before Judge Carroll calls for silence. I risk the glare of the flashbulbs to scan the room for the Kydd. After keeping vigil with me all weekend, he is not here for the reading of the verdict. Just as well. Someone from the office should get some sleep.

The first light of day illuminates the jurors as they file through the side door behind Charlie. Their faces are drawn; their eyes on the floor. Judge Carroll calls the case name and docket number. Normally, Wanda makes that announcement, but she doesn't work on Memorial Day, and she doesn't work at dawn on any day.

Judge Carroll's voice is thin and exhausted. "Ladies and gentlemen of the jury, have you reached a verdict?"

Juror number seven, the Postmaster from Wellfleet, stands, written verdict slip in hand. "We have, Your Honor."

Judge Carroll reaches toward him without comment. Charlie retrieves the folded verdict slip and carries it to the bench. Judge Carroll opens the form and reads, expressionless. Charlie returns the verdict slip to the Postmaster.

Harry tells his client to stand and face the jurors. Harry stands and faces them too. Rodriguez stares at each of the twelve jurors in turn. Not one of them meets his eyes.

Finally, Judge Carroll speaks again. "Mister Foreman, what say you?"

The Postmaster opens the verdict slip to read from it. His hands are shaking. "We, the jury, in the matter of *Commonwealth versus Rodriguez,* on the charge of murder in the first degree of one Michael Vincent Scott, do find the defendant, Manuel Rodriguez . . ."

Suspended animation.

"Guilty."

Bedlam.

My stomach knows what's happening long before my brain does. The smack of my skull against the counsel table is a noise I hear, but not a sensation I feel. I feel only his hands, callused, with jagged nails, around my neck. The photos of Michael Scott's smashed skull appear in my mind's eye.

I'm out of air. I can't swallow or blink. The tin codfish stares down at me. It is the only thing in the room, and it's spinning wildly.

Water everywhere. I'm soaked. I slide off the table and onto the floor. Air fills my lungs. Harry is beside me, lifting me, propping me up to a sitting position against the jury box. He is soaked too.

Rodriguez is cuffed and shackled on the carpeted floor. He, too, is drenched. Two court officers are on top of him. He forces his twisted face toward the photographers, pressing against the weight of an officer's shoulder, and shouts toward the reporters. "Hey, Madigan, way to go, man. I didn't kill that kid. But you damn near killed me. Attack your own goddamn client. Goddamn knocked me out. My own lawyer, man. Knocked me out."

The room is back in focus. An empty metal water pitcher is on the carpet in front of the judge's bench. Harry used it, I realize, on Rodriguez. Somehow, Harry got to him before the court officers did.

Judge Carroll is on his feet issuing directions, but I can't hear him above the ruckus from the gallery. Rodriguez's kids are crying; people are yelling. But Rodriguez is louder than anybody. "You got the wrong guy," he's shouting at the Scotts. "You got the wrong goddamn guy."

The court officers are staring up at the judge, shaking their heads, disgusted. They will have to transport Rodriguez to Cape Cod Hospital for evaluation. Since he claims he lost consciousness, they don't have a choice. He knows the system better than any of us.

The court officers drag Rodriguez toward the side door and he lets them, smiling at the members of the press as if he were enjoying the ride. As he passes the jury box, he looks down at me and laughs. "You'll get yours, bitch," he says.

The cameras get it all.

CHAPTER 11

Rob Mendell could have been President of the United States. The DA has the dark good looks of a film star; he is a polished public speaker, and he knows how to manipulate the media. Thirty minutes into the press conference on the front steps of the Superior Court-house, he answers each repetitious question as if the reporter asking it had shown keen insight. Woody Timmons, the regular courthouse reporter for the *Cape Cod Times,* has written Rob's words—"small town triumphs over big crime"—across his notepad. It will probably be tomorrow morning's headline.

The reporters don't yet know that Rob has accepted a partnership offer from a high-powered criminal defense firm in Hyannis, the "big city" of Cape Cod. He'll leave his position as Barnstable County's District Attorney when his current term expires in December. That's when Geraldine Schilling hopes to take over as Barnstable County's first female District Attorney. She has dedicated her entire adult life to that cause, forsaking all aspects of private life for a carefully calculated public persona.

Geraldine is aglow. The Rodriguez conviction is one she can point to again and again in her upcoming campaign. She will be the candidate whose small Cape Cod office has proven it can handle big-time crime. Earlier in this press conference, she all but announced her candidacy, even referred to me at one point as the next First Assistant. I had always assumed Geraldine would bring someone in from the outside to fill that post. Someone more politically savvy. Someone more like herself.

My adrenaline is beginning to wane. My briefcase is heavy and my knees are weak. Any strength I had left this morning was sapped by my final moments with Manuel Rodriguez. And my neck is suddenly out-throbbing my head.

A small crowd is gathering behind the press corps, despite the early hour. A squad car pulls up behind the crowd, lights flashing but siren mute. My stomach knots when the Kydd emerges from the passenger side. He removes his sunglasses and squints up the hill, directly at me. No grin.

Rob is entertaining the reporters with a war story, an anecdote from a case he tried years ago. No one pays any attention when I slip away. I take the granite steps two at a time, and I am winded when I reach the street. The Kydd leans close to me. There are beads of sweat on his brow. His hands are shaking and he is panting, as if he just finished running a marathon.

"Marty, they couldn't reach you. They couldn't reach anybody. Not Rob. Not Geraldine. So they got me."

"Who got you?"

"Chatham P.D."

"Why?"

"There's another one."

"Another one what?"

"Another murder. In Chatham. Body found on Harding's Beach at sunrise. Young white male. Slashed."

CHAPTER 12

Jeff Skinner has called a crew of medical technicians in on the holiday, and they are hard at work when I reach Harding's Beach. They have already identified the victim; no forensics were necessary. It's Skippy Eldridge, a nineteen-year-old local kid home on leave from the Air Force Radar Station at Otis Air National Guard Base on the Upper Cape. His Otis Air cap is blood-soaked, wedged between the back of his head and the beach.

Skippy's parents, Chuck and Emily, run a market at the Chatham Fish Pier. They keep an outboard in Oyster River and a few dozen lobster pots offshore. Skippy was probably on his way to check the pots this morning when he pulled off at Harding's Beach to enjoy his morning coffee and newspaper. Both items were found undisturbed on the dashboard of his pickup. Chief of Police Tommy Fitzpatrick is on his way to the Fish Pier to break the news to Skippy's folks.

It's clear to me at once that the only evidence to be gathered from this scene is on the ravaged corpse. The wind and the tide have claimed whatever information might have been left on the beach. Jeff's technicians are ready to bag the body, but they pause so that I can study it. I diagram the bloody remains of Skippy Eldridge in my notepad, careful to detail the position of each limb, the angle of the bloody torso, neck, and head, the narrow slice in his throat.

Skippy Eldridge. He'll always be nineteen now.

"Go ahead," I say. "You can take him."

There is a small shanty about the size of a tollbooth at the entrance to the Harding's Beach parking lot. It's used to collect parking fees during the summer season. It was scheduled to open today for the first time this year, but it won't. Instead, Chatham police are using it as part of a blockade, stopping the townspeople as well as the tourists from approaching the crime scene. Cars and trucks are backing up on Harding's Beach Road. Word is out.

The police clear a path for the county van carrying Skippy's remains. I ease the Thunderbird in behind it and head back to the office.

Rob and Geraldine are holding their second press conference of the day when I turn in to the Barnstable County Complex. This time they are standing on the front steps of the District Courthouse. I can hear Rob's voice from my reserved space in the parking lot, assuring the press that there is no connection between last year's murder and this one, that the police have multiple leads and are pursuing all of them, that his office will see to it that the perpetrator of this heinous crime is brought to justice.

Standing with Rob and Geraldine on the steps of the District Courthouse is Norman Richardson, the Executive Director of the Chatham Chamber of Commerce. Norman is visibly agitated, shifting from one foot to the other, shaking his head, and running his hands through his thinning hair every two minutes or so. Homicides wreak havoc with the tourist industry.

When Geraldine spots me, she pulls herself away from the cameras, a sure sign that whatever she's about to tell me is important. She catches up with me at the side entrance to the courthouse and lights a cigarette. "Martha, we need you at that autopsy."

This is Geraldine the politician speaking. I roll my eyes at her. "Geraldine, no one needs a prosecutor at an autopsy."

"We sure as hell do, Martha. You need to be there. Our office needs firsthand knowledge of this thing every step of the way."

"We'll know all there is to know when we get Jeff Skinner's report, Geraldine. I never understand what I'm looking at during those things anyway."

Geraldine actually blocks my entrance to the building. "I don't care if you understand what the hell you're looking at, Martha. Rob's got all he can handle with the press. I'm fielding phone calls from every goddamned hotel on Cape Cod. They're all reporting unexplained cancellations. Tourists are fleeing. This office has got to do something. And we've got to do it now."

CHAPTER 13

Jeff Skinner runs a tight ship. Two of the technicians who were on Harding's Beach earlier—one male, one female—are here to assist him with the autopsy. Both look too young—too innocent—to be so at ease in the presence of violent death. They move quietly and methodically about the spotless room, arranging instruments and documenting a chart with Skippy's name on it. It's business as usual, Memorial Day or not.

At precisely high noon, the male technician wheels the draped remains of Skippy Eldridge into the autopsy room. All living bodies in the room are dressed in green surgical suits, even mine. Jeff issues quiet directives to his two young assistants. I do my best to stay out of the way.

Just about everything in this room is made of polished stainless steel. The surgical instruments gleam. Bright fluorescent overheads beam down on the draped corpse. The antiseptic glare makes my eyes ache so much that I actually forget about my sore neck for a while.

It occurs to me as I watch Jeff scrub his arms up to the elbows that this is the second consecutive Memorial Day he has spent this way. Last year, when Michael Scott was killed, Jeff had been scheduled to be the keynote speaker at the Memorial Day ceremonies held annually at Chatham's single traffic rotary, Veterans' Circle. Hundreds of Chatham citizens attend those ceremonies each year, including dozens of veterans in uniform. The participants assemble at the rotary and walk in reverent procession to four downtown memorials honoring those Chatham natives who died in our nation's wars.

Chief of Police Tommy Fitzpatrick always leads the procession on motorcycle. Following behind him are the uniformed veterans, the color guards from the Chatham VFW Post, the U.S. Coast Guard Station Chatham, the 25th Battalion of the U.S. Marines, and all of the boys and girls who are Chatham Scouts. The civilians bring up the rear.

Last year, when the selectmen chose Jeff Skinner as the speaker, it was the first time a Vietnam veteran had been selected for the honor. But when Michael Scott's body was found, Jeff bowed out and came in to do the autopsy instead. A World War II veteran filled in for him.

Jeff finishes washing, moves to the gurney, and nods to one of his assistants, who presses the "record" button on a small tape recorder. Jeff identifies himself, gives the date and time, and identifies the other three of us in the room. He tells the little black box that he is about to begin the autopsy of Steven "Skippy" Eldridge. He adjusts the overhead lamp above the corpse and removes the drape with one practiced, fluid motion.

I am the only one in the room who gasps. Surely the others see it too. Skippy's body has been cleaned. The blood that covered his torso this morning is gone, and the knife wounds are clear. He is sliced open from his right shoulder to his left, from his right hip to his left, with two long incisions running vertically from shoulders to hips.

The knife wounds on Skippy Eldridge's chest form the Roman numeral II.

CHAPTER 14

"Of course you told them. Who the hell tries a murder-one case without describing the knife wounds?"

Geraldine is pacing around Rob Mendell's office, blowing smoke at the ceiling.

Rob's office is spacious, at least by Barnstable County standards, and he has decorated it handsomely. The walls are lined with framed photographs of Rob shaking hands and smiling with state legislators, judges, news anchors, and even a handful of movie stars. A soft leather couch, burgundy, sits against the far wall, with two matching chairs facing it. The same burgundy dominates the Oriental rug covering most of the old wooden floor.

At the opposite end of the room, Rob sits in the tall leather chair behind his great mahogany desk, holding his glasses in one hand and rubbing his eyes with the other. His suit coat hangs on the back of his chair and his starched white sleeves are rolled up to his elbows. I am slumped in one of the two chairs that face him. Geraldine, of course, won't sit down.

I have been awake—and wearing the same dark blue suit—for about thirty hours. I'm no match for her now. "Geraldine, I know I described the knife wounds. But I'm almost certain I never compared them to a Roman numeral. I didn't think that comparison was very clear from the photographs we had in evidence."

"But you probably mentioned it at some point during the week. And some copycat nut got wind of it. It's no more complicated than that."

"I don't think so, Geraldine." I'm getting nowhere here, and I need to go home. I need to hug Luke. I need to sleep.

Rob clears his throat. "Marty, Geraldine is probably right. But we'll order the trial transcript. That way you can check for yourself."

"The trial transcript?" Geraldine is beside herself. She leans across Rob's desk and stubs out her cigarette in the ashtray he keeps there for her use. "Martha's going to spend her time poring over a trial transcript? We have a murder to investigate, Rob. The tourist season is on top of us. We need this thing solved—fast. Who do you want me to put on it while Martha here reads the trial transcript? The Kydd?"

Geraldine lights another cigarette, collects herself, and speaks to me in a decidedly quieter voice. "Look, Martha, what if you didn't mention it? What if you just described the location of the wounds, and some nut made the connection to a Roman numeral one all by himself? Then the nut looks at his calendar, sees it's Memorial Day again, and it's irresistible. He makes his job as similar as he can—in Chatham, on the beach, young man—and he labels his guy with a Roman numeral two. Now, in his twisted little mind, he's more than just a nutcase. He's a nutcase with some kind of link to the first nutcase, who's already in jail."

I can't argue anymore, so I stand up and head for the door. "You're probably right, Geraldine. Like Rob says, you're probably right. All I know for sure is I've got to go home."

I am in the doorway when Rob stops me. "Marty," he says, "until we get a handle on this thing, it's probably best if you don't mention this to anyone else."

"Don't worry, Rob. I'll leave the press to you and Geraldine."

Geraldine moves into the doorway beside me and exhales smoke through her nostrils. Her green eyes are ablaze. "It's not just the press you should leave to us, Martha. Don't repeat one word of what you said here to anyone. Not anyone."

CHAPTER 15

Rodriguez strangles me again and again on the Monday night eleven o'clock news. It's the lead story. Skippy Eldridge's murder is second. The Dr. Wu case comes in third.

Luke is silent as he watches his father chat comfortably with reporters upon his arrival at the Seattle-Tacoma International Airport. Luke is always silent when Ralph is on television. When the interview is over, Luke will utter just one word. It's the same word after every interview.

"Psychobabble," he says.

Luke knew Skippy Eldridge only casually, but he is badly shaken by his death, badly shaken by the incomprehensible fact that a young man from Chatham—not Chicago or New York, but Chatham—has been murdered. We've spent most of the evening talking about Skippy, but now Luke turns his attention to the footage of Rodriguez's courtroom attack and takes a closer look at my neck. It's black and blue.

"Geez, Mom, Rodriguez could've killed you. What the heck were the guards doing? Why didn't they shoot him?"

"Shoot him? There were wall-to-wall people in that room. They couldn't open fire in there."

"I'd have shot him."

Luke has always been quick to dispose of the criminals I prosecute.

"This is the United States of America," I tell him. "That's not the way we do things."

What we will do is charge Rodriguez with assault and battery and assault with intent to murder. I'll do it personally in the morning. The charges will be meaningless in any practical sense. The murder-one conviction will keep Rodriguez behind bars for the rest of his natural life. But I intend to file them anyway.

I turn my attention back to my renegade son. "I'll shoot you," I tell him, "if you don't get to bed. Tomorrow's a school day."

Luke groans, but comes dutifully across the room to kiss me good night.

We exchange a short litany every night. It started years ago, when Luke was seven. It was a frigid day in March and Cape Cod was buried under two feet of snow. Winds were just short of hurricane velocity. The power was out and the roads were closed. Luke and I lit candles and kerosene lamps, and we warmed soup on the wood stove. We read stories by candlelight. It was a magical day.

When I tucked Luke in that night, I thanked him for helping me get through our first Cape Cod blizzard. His dark blue eyes sparkled with the earnestness only little boys own and he said, "Mommy, I'll always help you. And I'll always love you. And those two things will always be true."

I won't ever forget it. Every night since then, at bedtime, I tell him,

"Luke, I'll always help you. And I'll always love you. And those two things will always be true."

In recent years, Luke has been quick to point out that I can no longer help him with his math. But every night he smiles and says it back. Tonight is no exception.

I watch him climb the stairs with Danny Boy on his heels. My heart aches for Sally Scott and Emily Eldridge. They have lost their boys. For them, there will be no more good nights.

CHAPTER 16

Tuesday, June 1

The telephone has been ringing a long time in my dream. I awaken like a diver coming reluctantly to the surface. It's light already and the birds are chirping; the clock says five forty-five. Luke is standing in my room in a pair of old sweatpants, telling me patiently to pick up the receiver. Phone calls this early are always for me.

It's Rob.

"Marty, I'm sorry to call so early, but I thought you'd want to know. They've made an arrest in the Eldridge murder. The Chief says they picked up Eddie Malone."

Eddie Malone is a forty-four-year-old shell fisherman who is no stranger to Barnstable County prosecutors. Until now, though, his crimes have been relatively minor—barroom brawls, petty theft, drunk and disorderly. Eddie Malone has never struck me as a man who has the stomach for cold-blooded murder.

"Eddie Malone? This is out of his league, don't you think, Rob?"

"Two witnesses saw him fleeing the scene. And the forensics are solid. Malone's got the victim's blood all over his pant cuffs, socks, and shoes."

Well, what do you know. Eddie Malone's gone big time. I underestimated him.

"Anyhow, Marty, you should get here soon if you want to beat the press. They'll be swarming all over the complex in another hour."

"I'm on my way."

I put the phone back on my bedside table and give Luke a thumbs-up. "We've got him."

CHAPTER 17

Harry Madigan is waiting in my office. He's a good-looking man, six feet or so and powerfully built, with a ruddy complexion and charcoal-colored hair just beginning to gray at the temples. Harry stands and looks at me for a minute—he's been doing that lately—before he says anything. My cheeks are crimson by the time I reach my desk. The curse of the fair-skinned.

Harry always looks tired and a bit rumpled; his suit coat is usually wrinkled and his tie is always askew. Geraldine claims he sleeps for a few hours in his suit right before coming to work. Harry's disheveled appearance annoys Geraldine, and she always makes a point of telling him so. I find it somewhat endearing, and that annoys Geraldine even more. Today he looks worse than usual.

"Marty, what's going on? Eddie Malone? He's not up to this."

"That was my first thought too, Harry. But the police have eyewitnesses and the lab's got matches. Blood. Apparently all over your guy. It looks like your friend Eddie has moved up in the world."

Malone will be arraigned later today, as soon as we finish with the regular docket. As usual, Harry is right on top of it. He hands me all of the standard defense motions. But he doesn't leave. He stays planted in front of my desk, staring at me. "Marty, something's wrong here."

"What?" My stomach tightens even as I ask the question.

Harry is looking me straight in the eyes, as if he hopes to see a printout of my thoughts in them. "This doesn't add up," he says. "Chatham hasn't had two murders like this in its history. Now it's got two back to back. One year apart. Memorial Day. There are brains involved here somewhere. Rodriguez? Maybe. Malone? No way."

There are defense attorneys who come to my office to argue about every case they handle. Harry isn't one of them. He's here because he's genuinely troubled. And he wants to know if I am troubled too.

Images of the two numbered torsos pass before my eyes. I am sorely tempted to tell Harry what I thought I saw at yesterday's autopsy. I hesitate initially because of Geraldine's admonition. But my final decision has nothing to do with Geraldine. I decide not to tell Harry for a far better reason.

Harry and I will both receive copies of Jeff Skinner's final autopsy report. It will probably be on our desks late this afternoon. The report will include a half-dozen photographs, one of which the female technician took at my request, from a height of eighteen inches directly above the torso.

Harry may be inattentive to his wardrobe, but he never misses a detail in his examination of evidence. If there's a Roman numeral on Skippy Eldridge's chest, Harry will see it.

I look up at him with what I hope is a blank expression and shrug. "What can I say, Harry? Eyewitnesses. Blood. It's science."

Chapter 18

The Barnstable County District Courthouse is a drab, plain box of a building. It is as dull as the Superior Courthouse is striking. The Superior Court handles five hundred serious cases each year—murders, rapes, kidnappings, and arsons—while the District Court processes five hundred mundane offenses each week. In addition, all arraignments are held in the District Court, even those on charges that will ultimately be tried in Superior Court. Eddie Malone will be arraigned here later today.

The large waiting area outside the courtroom smells like a barroom after a weekend with its windows closed. Three nights' worth of arrestees are here to face their sins. The offenses range from street fights to narcotics possession, with no shortage of drunk driving and domestic violence charges mixed in. Lawyers and clients confer in hushed tones in every available corner.

Like its more elegant sister, the District Courthouse also has only one courtroom. This one, though, is large and dreary. Cheap paneling runs from the floor to the elevated ceiling, where dozens of cylindrical fixtures hold floodlights, a third of which are burned out. There is not a window in the room.

More cheap paneling covers the front and sides of the judge's bench as well as the courtroom clerk's desk in front of it. Counsel tables are stained dark brown and each has too many olive green, imitation leather chairs pulled up to it. Spectator pews are also dark brown, and many are adorned with the initials of those enterprising souls who managed to smuggle their Swiss army knives past the metal detector.

Every inch of the large courtroom is needed to contain the sea of humanity that converges here after a holiday weekend. The Kydd and I are handling this morning's docket together, and it will take both of us the better part of the day to get through the list.

The bailiff calls for order and Judge Richard Gould ascends to the bench. Judge Gould is a no-nonsense, get-the-job-done sort of judge, but he is admirably careful with the rights of the accused, both substantive and procedural. The appearance of his courtroom is not impressive, but the caliber of the proceedings conducted here is. It is Judge Gould who keeps the morning docket from resembling a cattle call. He treats each defendant who stands before him with fundamental fairness and respect.

Dottie Bearse has been the courtroom clerk here for decades, longer than any judge has lasted. She calls out the name of each defendant and, one by one, each walks to the microphone at the front of the room. Court officers are lined up against the back wall, where the doors are, just in case any one of them happens to walk in the wrong direction.

Each defendant who is represented by counsel stands mute as his attorney waives reading of the charges, enters a not guilty plea, and chooses a date a month or so off for a pretrial conference. Between now and then, the defense attorney will call or drop by our offices in an attempt to "work something out." If the charge is nonviolent and the defendant's record is halfway decent, a deal usually can be struck. In the meantime, most of these defendants are released on their own recognizance.

Then there are the defendants who are not represented. Judge Gould interrogates each of these individuals to determine whether or not the accused wants an attorney, and if he does, whether or not he can afford one. Each defendant who is able to pay for a lawyer is given a short continuance, during which he is expected to hire one. Those defendants found to be indigent are assigned to the "lawyer of the day"—usually an attorney newly admitted to the bar—who is on hand in the courtroom expressly for this purpose. These cases are held over for a second call, so that the lawyer of the day can confer with his new clients for at least a few minutes before proceeding.

Every once in a while we see a defendant who does not have a lawyer, does not want a lawyer, and intends to plead guilty on the spot. Almost always this is a person with an unblemished record who feels a tremendous combination of embarrassment and remorse over whatever lapse in judgment resulted in his arrest. He wants to face his punishment, and he doesn't want any delay. When I trained the Kydd to handle the morning docket, I told him to think of these people as kamikazes, catapulting headlong into sentencing without the benefit of counsel. I always recognize a kamikaze when I see one.

Today's kamikaze is Ernie Thompson, a fifty-year-old landscaper from Chatham who has been in the courthouse only once before, when he was called for jury duty. It seems Ernie arrived home from work a little early on Saturday and found his wife, Bess, in the marital bed with another man. To make matters worse, Bess's paramour turned out to be a competing landscaper, a young upstart whose business had just underbid Ernie's for a large job at the Chatham Bard's Inn, the grand old lady of Chatham's many fine hotels.

While the youthful Romeo struggled to pull on his pants, Ernie knocked him down and literally kicked him through the house and out the door. Then Ernie kicked him down the front steps, along the full length of his shell driveway, and into the road. As fate would have it, Romeo rolled into the road just as a Chatham squad car drove by.

I hand Ernie Thompson's file to the Kydd. Ernie and Bess are people I bump into around town every once in a while, at the grocery store or the gas station, and I'd just as soon not be the prosecutor on this one. The Kydd lives in Brewster, two towns away from Chatham; better that he handle it. Besides, Ernie is already mortified, and having a woman read these charges would only make him feel worse.

The Kydd struggles to contain his grin as he reads through the police report. Dottie Bearse calls Ernie's name and docket number and Ernie walks stiffly to the microphone, hat in hand.

The Kydd stifles his final grin and stands to address the court. "Your Honor, Mr. Thompson is charged with assault and battery with a dangerous weapon, to wit, a shod foot."

Judge Gould looks up from his paperwork to address Ernie. "Mr. Thompson, do you have an attorney?"

"No, sir."

"Do you want one?"

"No, sir."

"Mr. Thompson, you're charged with assault and battery with a dangerous weapon, potentially a very serious matter. Are you sure you don't want an attorney?"

"I'm sure, sir."

"Do you understand that a prison sentence is possible here, Mr. Thompson? I'm not saying it's a given, just that it's possible."

"I understand that, sir."

"And you're certain you don't want an attorney?"

"I'm certain, sir."

"And how do you intend to plead, Mr. Thompson?"

"Guilty, sir."

The judge turns a frustrated look on the Kydd. "All right, Mr. Kydd, let's hear the facts."

The Kydd has the police report in hand, but he doesn't read from it. "Your Honor, may I approach the bench?"

Judge Gould is annoyed at first, but after a moment he relents. "All right, Mr. Kydd. Make it quick."

The Kydd walks to the bench and hands the police report to the judge, whispering something I can't decipher. He returns to the counsel table without the report and recites the facts, but only from the driveway forward. "It seems there was an altercation between Mr. Thompson and the victim, during which Mr. Thompson knocked the victim to the ground and kicked him some distance, down a shell driveway and into the road, where Officer Trethaway saw them. You have the officer's report in front of you, Your Honor."

Judge Gould peers down at the report through dark-rimmed glasses, runs a hand over his mouth, and looks back at the Kydd.

"Mr. Thompson's record is clean, Your Honor, and the Commonwealth would be satisfied with a continuance without a finding for six months, if Mr. Thompson is agreeable."

Judge Gould's eyes linger on the Kydd a few moments before he looks at me for confirmation. I nod, and the judge turns his attention back to Ernie.

"Mr. Thompson, I'm inclined to follow the Commonwealth's recommendation here. I'd like to continue your case for six months without making any finding. If, at the end of six months, you haven't had any other run-ins with the law, these charges will be dismissed, and your clean record will be preserved. Is that agreeable?"

Ernie looks around before answering, as if he expects to see his guardian angel hovering nearby. "Yes, sir, I'll agree to that."

"Now I caution you, Mr. Thompson, any infraction during the next six months will result in your being sentenced immediately on this assault charge. Do you understand that?"

"Yes, sir. I do."

"All right, then, this matter is continued without a finding for six months. Mr. Thompson, you're free to go."

Ernie hustles toward the courtroom doors, as if he fears the judge will change his mind if he lingers. The Kydd winks at me as he sits down at the counsel table.

It was humane, what he did. He got the explanation for the assault in front of the judge without uttering a word of it out loud. And he gave Ernie the best deal he could. Ernie wouldn't have done any better if the best lawyer in New England had defended him.

I lean over and whisper to him. "You're a decent human being, Kydd."

He grins.

"Geraldine would never approve."

He laughs out loud.

It's after two o'clock by the time we finish the second call. The morning crowd has been replaced with reporters and spectators anticipating the Eddie Malone arraignment, jockeying for position even before Malone arrives. Dottie asks the judge if he'll break for lunch before this one, but he looks out at the full gallery and shakes his head.

Dottie reaches for Eddie's file and waits patiently for the noise in the gallery to subside. When all is quiet, she calls out the docket number and announces: *The Commonwealth of Massachusetts versus Edmund Joseph Malone.*

CHAPTER 19

Eddie Malone is a regular here. Normally, the court officers rib him about his antics when they escort him from lockup to the large court-room. More often than not, they are all laughing out loud when they spill through the side door. If the judge is already on the bench, they are quick to signal one another to quiet down.

But not today. Eddie and the two guards escorting him are stone-faced and silent when they enter the courtroom. The officers keep their eyes on the floor, even when a controlled murmur emanates from the crowd. Eddie looks up, though, and flashbulbs catch him from every angle. He looks like a deer caught in oncoming headlights.

Harry is at Eddie's side. The guards remove Eddie's cuffs and shackles, and Harry guides him toward the defense table. Eddie starts talking out loud as soon as his cuffs are off, as if the guards removed a muzzle as well. The whole room can hear every word, but Harry makes no attempt to stop him. The reporters are scribbling.

"Mr. Madigan, you ain't gonna send me up there, are you? I dint do it. I swear to God."

Harry puts his hands on Eddie's shoulders and leans over to whisper to him. Judge Gould pounds his gavel and the room grows still. I'm on.

"Your Honor, Mr. Malone is charged with murder in the first degree on the grounds of extreme atrocity or cruelty."

"I dint do it, Judge."

I turn and give Eddie my menacing look.

"The body of the victim, Steven Eldridge, was found by a man and woman who were jogging on Harding's Beach in Chatham at approximately five o'clock yesterday morning. They told police that they both screamed when they came upon the body, whereupon a man matching the description of this defendant emerged from the dunes nearby and fled. The couple reported that the man who fled appeared to have been awakened by their screams."

"That's right. I was sleepin', Judge. I was sound asleep. There ain't no law against sleepin', is there?"

I glare at him again.

"When police officers returned to the scene at approximately three o'clock this morning, they found Mr. Malone asleep in the dunes in precisely the spot where the couple first saw the man who fled, approximately ten yards from where the corpse was found."

"I sleep there a lot, Judge. There ain't usually a corpse there."

This time I glare at Harry; he stares back at me, his expression blank. I turn my back to him, walk to the bench, and hand the judge a copy of the police report. "Both the man and the woman—in separate lineups held this morning—identified this defendant as the man they saw fleeing the crime scene yesterday."

I stay close to the bench and hand the judge a copy of Jeff Skinner's preliminary report. "The Medical Examiner's preliminary report indicates that the victim sustained blunt trauma to the skull and multiple stab wounds, including perforation of the throat and larynx, which is believed to be the primary cause of death."

"I never done nothin' like that, Judge. I been in front of you lots of times, you know that, but I ain't never done nothin' like that."

I give up; I don't even bother to look his way.

"The report also indicates that blood matching that of the victim— and not matching that of the defendant—was found on the cuffs of this defendant's trousers, as well as on his socks and sneakers."

"I tripped, Judge. I musta tripped. That's all I can think."

"Your Honor, the Commonwealth asks that the defendant be held over for trial without bail."

Judge Gould peers over the dark rims of his glasses. "And the weapons, Ms. Nickerson? The blunt object? The knife?"

"At this time, Your Honor, no weapon has been found. The police continue to search the Harding's Beach area."

Judge Gould turns his attention to Harry. "Mr. Madigan, how does your client plead?"

Harry stands and hands me new paperwork. "Not guilty, Your Honor."

He hands a copy to the judge. "Not guilty by reason of insanity."

A low rumble erupts in the gallery. Eddie Malone is yelling out loud now. "Mr. Madigan, I ain't insane. I told you I ain't insane."

Judge Gould pounds his gavel. Reporters head for the doors, some already barking into their cell phones. Judge Gould keeps pounding. Harry doesn't even try to be heard until the court officers escort some of the noisier onlookers out of the room. Eventually, a hush falls over those who remain, all but Eddie Malone. He keeps yelling. "I ain't insane, Mr. Madigan. I ain't insane, and I ain't no killer."

Harry ignores him. "Your Honor, the defense moves, pursuant to Massachusetts General Laws chapter 123, section 15, that the defendant be committed to Bridgewater State Hospital for the statutory twenty-day observation period. We ask that the defendant be examined as to his competency to stand trial, as well as his mental state and level of criminal responsibility at the time he allegedly committed this crime."

Eddie is really upset now. "Mr. Madigan, don't send me up there. I ain't nuts. I ain't nuts, and I dint kill nobody. I swear to God."

Still, Harry ignores him.

"Your Honor, routine lab testing indicates that Mr. Malone's blood alcohol level at the time of his arrest was approximately point one nine. He's unable to recall substantial portions of the past forty-eight hours, including the hours immediately before and after the estimated time of the victim's death. I have serious concerns about Mr. Malone's ability to participate in a meaningful way in his own defense."

"I'm gonna participate," Eddie yells out. "Of course I'm gonna participate. I never said I wasn't gonna participate."

Harry doesn't even look at him. "In addition, Your Honor, the defense maintains that Mr. Malone suffers from an underlying mental defect. We need to determine what impact his alcohol consumption had on that defect. We need to know whether or not he had the capacity to appreciate the wrongfulness of his alleged conduct."

Eddie's still shouting. "There ain't no defect, Mr. Madigan. I ain't got no defect. I just don't remember, that's all. If I'da killed somebody, I'd remember."

Judge Gould seems not to notice Eddie at all. "Ms. Nickerson, any objection?"

Harry is right, of course. In every first-degree murder case, the Commonwealth has the burden of proving the defendant's intent and knowledge at the time he committed the crime. If the defendant presents credible evidence of mental impairment, it's all but impossible to meet that burden, even if the underlying mental condition was triggered by voluntary intoxication or drug use.

I wait for Eddie Malone to take a breath. "The Commonwealth has no objection, Your Honor."

"All right, then. It's hereby ordered that the defendant, Edmund Joseph Malone, be remanded to the custody of Bridgewater State Hospital for the statutory twenty-day observation period. This matter is continued until three weeks from today. We'll reconvene on Tuesday, June twenty-second, at one o'clock, or as soon thereafter as possible. We'll address the competency issue at that time and move forward with arraignment, if that's appropriate."

The bailiff directs us to stand. Judge Gould escapes into his chambers. The metal clasps close quickly on Malone's cuffs and shackles. The guards usher him out the side door, Harry right behind him.

Eddie's still pleading his case. "Mr. Madigan, this ain't right. I dint kill nobody. I swear it."

Harry's still ignoring him.

I sit down at the counsel table and hold my head in my hands while the spectators filter through the back doors. I am vaguely aware that the Kydd is sitting next to me. He hadn't left after we finished the regular docket.

"Marty, are you okay?"

"Kydd, did Harry Madigan make any attempt to quiet his client during that hearing?"

"No," he says. "I thought that was odd."

"It's more than odd. Harry never tolerates courtroom outbursts like that. I've seen him silence the worst of them."

Maybe Eddie Malone does have a mental defect. Maybe that's why Harry let him go on and on. Or maybe what Eddie Malone has is a clear conscience. Maybe he was telling the truth, and Harry wanted us to hear it.

CHAPTER 20

Wednesday, June 2

Harry is sitting on the curb in front of my reserved parking spot when I pull in to the county complex. His briefcase is open on the little patch of grass beside him. His papers are a mess, but his clothes are worse. Lucky for him Geraldine isn't here yet.

I lean against the hood of the Thunderbird. Harry squints up at me in the morning sun.

"New office space, Harry?"

He laughs a tired laugh. "Budget cuts are hell," he says.

I sit down on the front fender, so I can look him in the eye. "Harry, why are you sitting here?"

He gives me that look again—it's a nice look, really—and I feel the damn color rising in my cheeks once more. Harry takes an envelope from the clutter in his briefcase and hands it to me. "This is why," he says.

The large square envelope is from the Medical Examiner's office and I know before I open it that it contains Jeff Skinner's final report on Skippy Eldridge. It must have been delivered after I left last night. Harry's copy is dog-eared already, and it is opened to one of the photographs of Skippy's lacerated chest, though not the one taken at my request.

After a moment Harry points to the sliced torso. "Remind you of anything, Marty?"

I get it now. Harry hasn't said anything about Roman numerals, but he sees the similarities between these wounds and Michael Scott's. He's sitting in the parking lot so that I can speak freely. No chance Geraldine or Rob will hear this conversation.

"They're knife wounds, Harry."

"They're not just knife wounds. They're specific cuts. Shoulder to shoulder. Hip to hip. Just like the Scott kid. Throw in a fractured skull and a slit throat and guess what, Marty? We've got identical murders. Identical Memorial Day murders."

Portions of the Scott file are in the backseat of the Thunderbird, including the eight-by-ten glossies that were not introduced at trial. One of them is the shot that comes closest to showing what looks like a Roman numeral I on Michael Scott's chest. It isn't as clear as it could be, though; it's taken from beside, not above, his body.

I pull the file from the back of the Thunderbird and slide the photo from its envelope. I flip through the Eldridge photos until I find the one I requested. Skippy's Roman numeral II is as vivid as I recall.

I sit down on the curb next to Harry and place the photographs side by side on the grass. "Not identical, Harry. There is a difference."

Minutes pass while Harry stares at one photograph, then the other. The expression on his handsome face is blank. I can actually feel a physical weight lifting from my shoulders. If Harry doesn't see it, then it isn't there. It's all in my head.

But Harry catches his breath, then checks both photos again. His ruddy complexion turns a deeper red. I can all but see his pulse racing. He closes his eyes, shakes his head, and stares at the photos yet again before turning his astonished face toward me.

"Jesus Christ, Marty. They're numbered."

CHAPTER 21

Thursday, June 3

"Set aside the verdict? It took all goddamned weekend to get a verdict. Why the hell should the judge set it aside?"

Geraldine is wearing out the Oriental rug in Rob's office.

Harry's motion to set aside the Rodriguez verdict was on my desk when I arrived this morning. I knew it would be. Harry classified it as an emergency motion and the clerk's notation indicates Judge Carroll will hear him at three o'clock, a half hour from now. I spent the morning drafting our written opposition, though I am ambivalent at best about our argument.

Rob isn't happy. Geraldine is enraged. She spent most of the day with Norman Richardson of the Chamber of Commerce, explaining the evidence we're assembling against Eddie Malone, so that Norman can calm the fears of Chatham's merchants and visitors. She learned of Harry's motion just moments ago and she realizes, as we all do, that the press will be all over it.

"He's arguing newly discovered evidence, Geraldine."

"Newly discovered evidence? A photograph he's had for more than a year? He calls that newly discovered evidence?"

"His argument is based on two photographs, Geraldine. One he's had for more than a year. The other he's had less than forty-eight hours."

Geraldine lights a new cigarette, though she still has one burning in the ashtray on Rob's desk. She inhales deeply and tilts her blond head to one side. I feel sarcasm coming on.

"And he's seeing numbers. Just like you did, Martha. You're both seeing numbers. But not just ordinary numbers. Oh no. Roman numerals. After all, this is Chatham we're talking about. No ordinary numbers. No ordinary town."

"Geraldine," Rob says, "knock it off. Marty didn't file the motion; Madigan did. She's just telling you what he's arguing."

Geraldine turns her back to Rob and leans against his desk. "And what about you, Martha? What are you arguing?"

"It's basically your argument, Geraldine. A subsequent copycat crime doesn't negate the original conviction. Anyone who read the newspaper or watched the evening news during the last week in May knew how Michael Scott was sliced. Any psychopath could mimic that crime."

For a split second it actually seems that Geraldine is going to hit me. She explodes. "Any psychopath? Any psychopath? No, Martha, not just any psychopath. A very specific psychopath. Malone. Remember him? He's the nutcase who killed Eldridge. He's locked up at Bridgewater right now so they can tell us just what kind of a nutcase he is. Did you forget that?"

"No, Geraldine, I didn't forget that. But I'm not trying to convict Malone today. I'm trying to keep Rodriguez in jail."

"You'd better convict Malone today, Martha. Every square inch of that courtroom will be covered with reporters, and you'd damn well better convict Malone in their eyes. If you don't, they'll be screaming from the rooftops about a serial killer on the loose. And there won't be a tourist left on Cape Cod."

I stand and take my briefcase from the edge of Rob's desk.

"I'm heading over," I tell them.

Rob and Geraldine are going too, of course. But I'd just as soon walk over alone, take a few minutes to collect my thoughts. I head toward Rob's office door. But Geraldine isn't finished.

"That should be your alternate argument, Martha. You realize that, don't you?"

"What do you mean, alternate?"

"There aren't any numbers, Martha. Just random gashes. The numbers only exist in Madigan's messy imagination. That should be your first response."

I turn and face those piercing green eyes. "I can't say that, Geraldine. I just can't say that."

CHAPTER 22

The Superior Courthouse is mobbed. Charlie calls for silence three times before the din subsides. Judge Carroll emerges from chambers and strides toward the bench, copies of Harry's motion and my opposition tucked under his arm in the folds of his robe. The stenographer is perched on the edge of her seat, fingers poised over her narrow machine.

Harry is on his feet, ready to address the court, but Judge Carroll raises a hand to stop him.

"I've read your motion, Mr. Madigan. I've read your motion and I've examined the two photographs you submitted to the court. I've also read the Commonwealth's response. Unless you have facts to add that aren't in your written materials, I'm prepared to rule."

Harry is taken aback. It is routine to allow the moving party to present his motion orally, to emphasize important points or clarify information that might be fuzzy otherwise. Yet Judge Carroll wants to rule without so much as a summary from Harry. The room actually falls silent for a minute, and during that time I realize what the judge is doing. So does Harry.

"I do, Judge," he says. "I do have facts to add to my written materials."

Judge Carroll purses his lips, clearly not happy to hear this. But he's stuck now. Harry has called his bluff.

"All right, Mr. Madigan. No need to rehash what I've already read. Just give me the additional facts."

Harry is on a slow simmer. He paces back and forth in front of the judge's bench. He turns and points toward the gallery, keeping his eyes on Judge Carroll. "Okay, Judge, here's an additional fact. This court is more concerned about these reporters than it is about a man wrongly convicted of murder."

The crowd erupts. Judge Carroll bangs his gavel. Charlie looks confused. Harry keeps talking.

"That's right, Judge. You don't want to hear my argument because you don't want the reporters to hear it."

Harry is steaming now. He takes a copy of his motion—complete with photographs—from his briefcase. He hands it to Woody Timmons, the reporter from the *Cape Cod Times,* who is seated in the front row. "There's a copy machine in the clerk's office," Harry tells him. Woody's expression is one Moses might have worn when God handed him the Ten Commandments.

Judge Carroll is standing, banging his gavel randomly on the bench. "Mr. Madigan, you're out of line."

"Am I, Judge? Am I out of line by pointing out to this court that whoever killed Michael Scott last Memorial Day also killed Steven Eldridge this Memorial Day? Why is that out of line, Judge? Because you don't want to hear it?"

Harry thrusts his fist toward the gallery. "Or because you don't want them to hear it?"

"That's enough, Mr. Madigan."

"No, it's not, Judge. It's not enough. There's more you don't want them to hear. You don't want them to hear that the victims have numbers carved on their chests."

The crowd's steady murmur turns into a roar. Harry raises his voice to be heard above it. "You don't want them to hear that Michael Scott had the number one etched into his body and that, even though no one ever pointed it out publicly, Steven Eldridge is in the morgue right now with the number two carved into his."

Harry draws the Roman numerals in the air with his index finger as he speaks. The crowd is out of control. So is Judge Carroll. I've never heard him shout before.

"Mr. Madigan, one more word and I'll hold you in contempt."

It's too late. Harry is at full boil.

"I hold you in contempt, Judge. I hold you in contempt for not giving a damn. When will you give a damn, Judge? Next Memorial Day? When the body in the morgue has a three on it?"

Judge Carroll signals the guards and all four of them surround Harry. They take his arms and he drops to his knees on the plush floral carpeting. If they want him out of the courtroom, they're going to have to drag him.

"Or maybe it'll be sooner than that, Judge. These sorts of people need to kill more and more frequently, don't they? Isn't that what the experts say? Maybe we'll see number three sometime soon."

Everybody is standing now. And everybody is yelling. But Harry is louder than anybody. He is bigger than any one of the guards, and they are having difficulty removing him.

"In the meantime, Judge, keep Manuel Rodriguez locked up like a dog. It makes everybody feel better."

Harry jerks his arm away from a guard who is trying to cuff him and thrusts his fist toward the gallery again. "That way these guys won't go nosing around where they shouldn't. Right, Judge? Protect that jury verdict, Judge, no matter what. Otherwise the whole god-damned system will unravel."

The guards drag Harry through the side door, and his words grow muffled and distant when it closes.

The reporters and photographers are gone, following Harry down the hallway, shouting questions at him. The courtroom is silent. Charlie Cahoon looks like he's a hundred years old. I am paralyzed.

Judge Carroll takes his seat and waits for the stenographer to regain her composure before he speaks. He is ashen. He looks at me without seeing me as he delivers his rulings. His voice is brittle.

"Mr. Madigan is in contempt of this court and will be held in custody until further notice. The motion to set aside the jury's verdict in *Commonwealth versus Rodriguez* is denied. Sentencing will go forward as scheduled on Monday, June seventh, at one o'clock. Until then, we are adjourned."

The judge is in chambers before a dazed Charlie Cahoon tells us to rise. Charlie disappears through the side door. Those spectators who remained after Harry was dragged away are filing out the back, whispering as if they just witnessed something holy.

My head is pounding. I sit down and lower it onto my arms on the counsel table. I look up when I feel a hand on my shoulder. It's Geraldine.

"Congratulations," she says. "You won."

CHAPTER 23

Charlie Cahoon agrees to let me into Harry's cell, but he isn't happy about it. "It's bad enough he's in there, Miss Marty. Now you want to go in there too?"

Charlie has called me "Miss Marty" since I was in elementary school with Jake.

"I just want to keep him company, Charlie."

"For how long? You gonna sit in there all night?"

"We'll both be out in an hour. Harry's office is working on it. Judge Carroll will release him as soon as everybody calms down."

Charlie pauses in the hallway in front of one of the empty cells and searches my eyes. His expression is pained. "Why did he do that? Harry's never done anything like that before. Why now?"

"He just lost his temper, Charlie. That's all."

"He believes what he said in there, doesn't he? About the numbers. He believes that."

"Yes," I tell him. "He believes that."

"And what about you, Miss Marty? Do you believe it?"

I lean against the bars of the empty cell and return his stare. "I don't know, Charlie. I don't know what to believe."

He shakes his head and resumes a slow shuffle toward Harry's cell. He puts his key in the lock and opens the door for me. Once I'm inside, he closes it slowly and locks it behind me. He wears a sad look as he turns away.

The truth is, there are a couple of questions I need to ask Harry. And a Superior Court holding cell is as safe a place as any to hear the answers. The other three cells are empty. The information won't go anywhere it shouldn't.

Harry is seated on a small cot that hangs from steel hinges attached to one concrete wall of the cell. His suit coat is rolled in a ball on the floor next to his feet, and his white shirt is drenched with sweat. He laughs when I sit down beside him.

"You know, Marty, I've been thinking about inviting you over to my place. But I didn't picture it quite like this."

I laugh too, my cheeks instantly on fire.

"Harry, I have a couple of questions for you."

"Shoot," he says.

"One of the things you said in court was that no one ever publicly mentioned that the Scott boy's wounds looked like a Roman numeral one. Are you sure about that?"

"Am I sure?"

"Are you sure I didn't say anything about that during the trial?"

"Marty, I had zero to work with in that case. If I'd had any clue that those cuts looked like a number, I'd have made something of it. Trust me."

He looks sideways at me and raises his eyebrows. "Next question?"

"This one's harder," I tell him. "I'm going to ask you to break a client confidence."

Harry closes his eyes, laughs again, and leans back against the concrete wall. "Do I look like a guy who would break the rules?"

He stays pressed against the wall, but eventually he turns his face toward me and opens his eyes. They're bloodshot.

"I wouldn't ask, Harry, if it wasn't important."

"Go ahead and ask. But I'm not promising an answer."

"I need to know why you made the theft argument."

"What?"

"The theft argument. Was that your story or your client's? You argued that Michael Scott was already dead, that Rodriguez just stole his watch and money. Did you raise that argument because it's all you could come up with? Or is that what Rodriguez told you?"

Harry doesn't hesitate. "That's what he told me, Marty. That's what he told me the first time I interviewed him, right after he was picked up. And he stuck to it. He never changed his story."

"Did you believe him, Harry?"

Harry leans forward again and stares at his shoes for a few minutes. He raises his head and meets my eyes.

"I do now," he says.

CHAPTER 24

Friday, June 4

Rob, Geraldine, and the Chamber of Commerce guy disappeared behind the closed door of Rob's office shortly after I got to work this morning. They were still there when the Kydd and I left to cover the morning docket. They emerge just as we return, a few minutes before twelve. The press conference is scheduled for high noon.

The Kydd and I head into the lunchroom, pour some coffee, and flip on the old television set that extends from the wall on a mechanical arm. *News at Noon* begins with a live shot in front of our building. Geraldine is front and center, with Rob and Norman Richardson on either side. She is smiling as if the events of the past twenty-four hours were all part of her plan, and she is eager to let those assembled in on her strategy.

Geraldine leans into the microphone, still smiling, but she doesn't say a word. After several minutes, the reporters fall silent, realizing she won't tell them anything until they do.

"Ladies and gentlemen, I'd like to make a very brief statement about yesterday's unfortunate display, and then the District Attorney, Rob Mendell, will address you.

"I'm quite sure that Mr. Madigan did what he did yesterday because he thought it would help his client. After all, that's Mr. Madigan's job. Fortunately for the rest of us, Judge Carroll did his job too.

"The awful truth here is that two young men were brutally murdered in a town that is unaccustomed to such atrocities. The good news is that both killers were apprehended quickly and both remain incarcerated. They no longer pose any danger to the law-abiding citizens of Chatham.

"Manuel Rodriguez murdered Michael Scott in cold blood, and this office saw to it that Rodriguez was convicted of that crime. He will be sentenced on Monday, just as he should be, regardless of Mr. Madigan's dramatic attempt to prevent that.

"Edmund Malone murdered Steven Eldridge in the same barbaric manner, and we'll make sure Malone is brought to justice too. As we speak, he is being evaluated at Bridgewater State Hospital. I'm sure you are all aware that Malone's own attorney, the very same Mr. Madigan who performed for us yesterday, requested that psychiatric assessment.

"If Malone is competent to stand trial, we assure you we will secure his conviction. If he is incompetent, he will remain institutionalized at Bridgewater or some comparable facility. Under no circumstances will Edmund Malone return to the streets, or the beaches, of Cape Cod.

"Both Michael Scott and Steven Eldridge died as the result of multiple stab wounds. Mr. Madigan's antics notwithstanding, the similarities end there.

"Now I'd like to turn the microphone over to our District Attorney."

"What about the Roman numerals, Ms. Schilling?" It's Woody

Timmons from the *Cape Cod Times,* the front-row recipient of Harry's written motion with photos.

Geraldine had stepped aside to make room for Rob, but she moves back toward the microphone. "There are no Roman numerals."

Woody holds up the photographs. "Sure look like Roman numerals to me," he says.

The reporters grow noisy again; Rob takes the microphone from its stand and walks closer to them. "Ladies and gentlemen, if I can have your attention, please. I have a rather important announcement to make."

I turn to the Kydd. "Here it comes."

"Here what comes?"

"Rob's stepping down."

"He's what?"

"Not now. In December, at the end of his term. But he's going to tell them now. And he's going to endorse Geraldine as his successor."

The Kydd looks a little bit hurt. "How come I never know what's going on around here?"

Rob has the crowd's attention.

"It has been my great honor to serve as the District Attorney of Barnstable County for three consecutive terms."

The reporters buzz. They weren't expecting this.

"I am proud of the work we've done in the past twelve years. I am proud of the role we've played in keeping the villages of Cape Cod safe for all who live and vacation here. But it's time for me to move on to the next phase of my life, to make way for my successor in this important office."

Rob gestures toward Geraldine and flashes a winning smile. "And I just happen to know who wants the job."

Everyone laughs at this, even Geraldine.

"Ms. Schilling has been my right-hand man . . ."

More laughter.

". . . for the past twelve years and I heartily endorse her candidacy for this office. There is no one more qualified; no one more experienced in the administration of justice; no one more committed to fighting the good fight."

It's brilliant. The timing of this announcement is nothing less than brilliant. Last night's news was dominated by scenes of Harry. Harry announcing that the victims are numbered; Harry asking Judge Carroll when he's going to give a damn; Harry dropping to his knees and predicting we'll see victim number three sometime soon. The viewing public might have thought no one else spoke yesterday in all of New England.

That won't happen again tonight. Between Geraldine's statement and Rob's surprise announcement, Harry will get a lot less airtime.

But Woody Timmons refuses the detour. "Ms. Schilling," he shouts above the ruckus, "Martha Nickerson from your office never said a word yesterday. What does she have to say about Roman numerals?"

Geraldine smiles indulgently at him. "Ms. Nickerson is a very capable trial attorney. She knows a red herring when she sees one."

"But what does she say about Roman numerals?"

Geraldine's smile grows tight at the corners. "She says what every rational person says. There are no Roman numerals."

The Kydd has been watching me instead of the television. "She's lying, isn't she, Marty?"

I punch him lightly on the arm, but I don't answer.

CHAPTER 25

Sunday, June 6

Ralph flew into the Chatham Municipal Airport this morning in a small chartered plane. He's here to take Luke to lunch. He'll fly out again this afternoon to Logan International in Boston, where he'll catch a commercial flight back to Seattle. His direct testimony in the Dr. Wu trial ended Friday. The prosecution will begin cross-examining him tomorrow.

Luke isn't happy. It's a crisp, sunny day and he'd rather be on the beach with Justin, Jake Junior, and the other guys than in a restaurant with his recently surfaced father. To make matters worse, Ralph announced when he called yesterday that he expects to finish up in Seattle later this week, and he wants to take Luke to a Vincent van Gogh exhibit at the Museum of Fine Arts in Boston next Sunday. Luke has been begging me to intercede.

In spite of his efforts during the past year, Ralph doesn't seem to know Luke much better now than he did when his visits began. Luke is an outdoors guy. In the winter, he plays basketball and goes skiing.

In the summer, he plays baseball and goes fishing. Spending a June Sunday in Boston instead of on Cape Cod is a penance. Spending it indoors is unthinkable.

Luke is still in the shower when Ralph arrives. I hand Ralph a mug of coffee and move the Sunday paper from the couch so he can sit. The television is tuned to *Cape Cod Sunday* and Geraldine is the featured guest. She is outlining the tenets of her campaign, her vision for minimizing violent crime in Barnstable County.

"Ralph," I begin, "about next Sunday."

Ralph sips his coffee. "The museum?"

"Right. I was thinking. Maybe instead of taking Luke to the museum, you could take him to a Red Sox game at Fenway Park. I checked the schedule. The Sox are playing the Yankees at five o'clock next Sunday."

Ralph scoffs at the idea. "Marty, you know I'm not a sports fan."

I want to tell him this isn't about him, but I don't. "I know that, Ralph, but Luke is. He's really much more of a ballpark kid than a museum kid."

Ralph wears a dark look as he considers this.

"Blame it on my side of the family," I tell him.

Luke clamors down the stairs and gives Ralph an awkward hello. Danny Boy is close behind, growling before he even sees Ralph.

Ralph frowns at Danny Boy, puts his coffee mug down, and looks up at Luke. "Luke, your mother tells me you'd rather go to the Red Sox game next Sunday. Is that right?"

Luke's face brightens and he gives me a surprised look. I hadn't mentioned the game to him. I didn't know if I'd be able to sell the idea to Ralph.

It takes a few moments for Luke to realize that Ralph is waiting for an answer. "Well, yeah, of course I would."

"Okay, then that's what we'll do."

Ralph stands and heads to the kitchen with his empty mug. As soon as he is out of sight, Luke gives me two thumbs up, a grateful smile, and a stage whisper. "Hey Mom, you're okay."

When Ralph returns, his eyes are drawn to the television screen, where the discussion has turned to the inevitable. The host questions Geraldine about the Chatham Memorial Day murders. Geraldine denies the existence of any evidence to suggest the two are related, after which the host, of course, shows footage from Thursday's scene in Judge Carroll's courtroom. Harry on his knees, giving the warning that most of the viewing public must have memorized by now.

". . . maybe it'll be sooner than that, Judge. These sorts of people need to kill more and more frequently, don't they? Isn't that what the experts say? Maybe we'll see number three sometime soon."

Ralph shoves both hands into his pants pockets and juts his bearded chin out toward Harry. "He's right, you know."

"Right about what?"

"About the killer striking sooner next time. He's gotten away with it twice. He's feeling empowered now."

I have always marveled at the certainty with which Ralph predicts the behavior of others. His words make me shiver.

"You're assuming these murders are the work of one killer."

A small smile crosses Ralph's lips, as if he just remembered my role in all of this. "That's right," he says. "I'm assuming these murders are the work of one killer."

Chapter 26

Monday, June 7

The fact that I own a gun startles me every time I think of it. It was not something I wanted. Geraldine insisted. I'd spend the rest of my days handling misdemeanors, she told me, unless I learned how to pack a piece.

That was more than eight years ago. Geraldine filled out the application for my permit to carry. She told me the permit would issue immediately, no questions asked, because of my profession. She told me she would chat with the guards at the county complex, after which they would routinely wave me around the metal detectors. She was right on both counts.

Geraldine went with me to buy the gun. She criticized my selection. My .32-caliber Lady Smith was a "sissy gun" she said, compared to her nine-millimeter Walther PPK. Nevertheless, she took me and my sissy gun to the firing range a dozen times for training. In the end, she said my shot wasn't half bad, a far better rating than I'd ever expected.

Geraldine said I should carry my gun with me at all times, just as she does. And I should visit the firing range at least once a month, just as she does. But, she said, if I chose instead to lock the Lady Smith in a closet, where it would do me no good, then so be it. She'd done what she could.

I carried it with me for a solid year. It fit easily into the interior pockets of my suit jackets. I got used to the small weight of it against my body. And I went faithfully to the firing range every month, just as Geraldine directed. I followed all of her directions that year. But then the Erickson matter came to our office.

Gordon Erickson was a tuna broker who lived in Truro. His refrigerated truck could be seen at harbors all over Cape Cod during tuna season. He would buy the large fish—many weighing more than six hundred pounds—directly from the boats of tuna fishermen. Then he'd truck them to Boston, where they'd be crated on ice and airlifted to Japan. Fresh tuna fetches a shockingly high price on the sushi market.

The commercial end of the fishing industry is dirty from top to bottom. Truro's Chief of Police didn't hesitate in approving Gordon Erickson's application for a permit to carry. Gordon was a lifelong Truro resident with nothing more than a few minor traffic infractions on his record. His permit remained in good standing for years, until one terrible morning in September, almost seven years ago.

It was a banner tuna season that year, and Gordon was driving to Boston daily. He drove back to Cape Cod late one September night in a pelting rainstorm. He'd been awake since before dawn that day. When he got home, he hung his jacket on a hook in the mud room, and went straight to bed.

The shots woke Gordon and his wife early the next morning. Their ten-year-old son had been looking for bubble gum in his dad's jacket pocket and found the loaded revolver instead. He pointed it at his seven-year-old sister and pulled the trigger twice. She was dead before the second shot hit her.

Luke had turned ten just two months earlier.

When I left work that day, I went straight to an office supply store and bought a metal strongbox with a secure lock. When I got home, I put the unloaded gun into the box, locked it, and stored it in the back of my closet. I put the ammunition in another strongbox, one already holding Luke's birth certificate, the deed to the Windmill Lane cottage, and the single insurance policy I purchased to provide for Luke if anything ever happens to me. I locked that one and stored it in the bottom of a dresser drawer.

I put the key to the first strongbox on the top shelf of the bathroom medicine cabinet. The key to the second box I stored on a top shelf in the pantry. Geraldine was right. The gun would do no good in the closet. But it would do no harm either.

Geraldine made the decision to charge Gordon Erickson with involuntary manslaughter. Rob was reluctant. After all, he told Geraldine, the man had already paid dearly for his carelessness. Ultimately, though, Rob acquiesced, the charge was issued, and trial was scheduled for the following February. But on Christmas Eve, after writing a long letter to his wife and son, Gordon Erickson went into the back of his refrigerated truck with his hunting rifle, the only firearm the Truro police had missed when they confiscated the rest. He put the barrel in his mouth and pulled the trigger.

I still go to the firing range a few times a year. And I keep up with routine maintenance on the Lady Smith. But I haven't carried it with me since the day the little Erickson girl died. Until today.

Manuel Rodriguez will be sentenced in an hour. I am no longer certain that he killed Michael Scott. But there is no doubt in my mind that he would have killed me if he could have. I can still feel his large, callused hands around my neck, preventing me from taking even the smallest sip of air. The Lady Smith probably wouldn't have made any difference in that incident. But it might if there's a next one.

I decided to tell Luke about the Lady Smith. I showed it to him this morning before I dropped him off at school. I explained my reasons for owning it as well as my decision to resume carrying it. I asked him to promise me that he will never touch it when I'm not around. He's sixteen now, almost seventeen. And he is mature beyond his years. I can rely on his word.

I used to worry that Luke seemed more mature than his peers. I worried that he lost too much of his childhood when Ralph and I divorced, that he was forced into the "man of the house" role far too soon. But in recent years that worry has left me, replaced by a genuine admiration for the fine young man he has become. His observations about the world around him and the people in it are thoughtful and kind. He is true and loyal to his friends.

Luke was surprised to learn that I own a gun. He was astonished to hear that I actually know how to use it. Without hesitation, he promised he'll never touch it. When I tucked it into my jacket pocket, he smiled at me.

"Hey, Mom," he said, shaking his head as if he were the parent, "stay safe."

CHAPTER 27

The sentencing itself is a nonevent. Rodriguez will be sentenced to life in prison without the possibility of parole. The sentence is mandated by statute for all those convicted of first-degree murder. The judge has no discretion.

The proceedings, on the other hand, promise to be dramatic.

Students and professors from Boston University fill the courtroom and the hallway. Michael Scott's roommates set an enlarged photograph of Michael—smiling in his baseball uniform—on an easel in front of the judge's bench. The entire college baseball team, in uniform, lines the back of the room. Players and coaches alike stand at attention, black bands on their upper right arms, caps held over their hearts. The press is salivating.

One of Michael Scott's parents will deliver a victim impact statement before Rodriguez is sentenced. I expect it will be his father. During the year that I have known the Scotts, Sally has been unable to complete a sentence about her murdered son. She broke down so often during questioning in my office, I relied solely on her husband for testimony during trial.

It is because of the victim impact statement that the Superior Courtroom and its loft are filled to capacity. An overflow crowd is in a first-floor conference room, where the proceedings will be broadcast on a closed-circuit monitor.

The Scott family is seated in the usual spot, with the Rodriguez family directly across the aisle, the two little curly-haired boys watching the side door for their father. Geraldine and Rob are side by side in two of the chairs reserved for attorneys, against a waist-high bar that separates them from the general public. The Kydd got stuck handling the docket alone in District Court this morning, but he arrives in Superior Court just in time. I signal for him to join me at the counsel table.

Harry is already at the defense table when the side door opens and Manuel Rodriguez comes in, cuffs and shackles in place and locked. Charlie told me when I arrived that Judge Carroll had directed the guards to keep Rodriguez restrained throughout sentencing, a precaution against the kind of outburst we saw when the verdict was returned. Even so, I am glad I decided to bring the Lady Smith along. The weight of it against my side is reassuring, though I would never fire it in this crowded courtroom.

Charlie calls for quiet and directs the crowd to stand. Judge Carroll emerges from chambers. Wanda calls the case name and docket number. When the rest of us sit down, Rodriguez and Harry remain standing.

Judge Carroll stares at Harry. Harry glares back at him. It's the first time the two men have faced each other since the judge threw Harry in jail. The photographers can't click fast enough. Minutes pass before Judge Carroll speaks.

"Mr. Madigan, you are entitled, of course, to make a statement on behalf of your client. But before you do, we are going to hear from a member of the Scott family."

Harry sits down without a word. Rodriguez sits too. The judge adjusts his bifocals, squints at a small piece of notepaper, and looks toward the courtroom's front row. "Mrs. Sally Scott, we will hear from you now."

There is a general stir in the room as Sally Scott rises from her seat and walks to the front of the courtroom. Instinctively, I stand when she reaches the counsel table. She takes my hands in hers. When I look in her eyes, I understand that she is about to do the most difficult thing she has ever done—speak in public about her slain son. I also understand that, for her, silence is not an option.

"Thank you, Attorney Nickerson," she says simply.

I feel a twinge of guilt, as if I double-crossed her somehow, but I say nothing. She walks calmly toward the judge's bench and stands beside Michael's photograph.

"Mr. Rodriguez, you are a coward." Sally's voice is surprisingly strong. She appears composed and steady. She is an attractive forty-eight-year-old, with thick auburn hair cropped extremely short. Her cheeks are flushed. She keeps her deep brown eyes on Rodriguez, though he refuses to look back at her.

"You attacked my son from behind, you coward. You smashed his skull before he ever saw you. You knifed him, and he was unarmed. And now, you won't look at his mother. You are a small, cowardly excuse for a man."

The chains on Rodriguez's cuffs bang the back of his chair as he shifts in his seat and glowers at the empty jury box.

"If you weren't such a coward, Mr. Rodriguez, Michael would be alive today. He was stronger and smarter than you will ever be. If you had faced him like a man, instead of ambushing him from behind, he would have broken you in two. And the world would be a far better place, Mr. Rodriguez, if Michael were still in it."

Sally Scott picks up the large photograph of Michael and carries it toward the jury box, trying to put it in Rodriguez's line of vision. I am more than a little surprised by her moxie.

"This is the young man you murdered, Mr. Rodriguez. You probably didn't know how handsome he was. You didn't look at his face, did you? I suppose that's one advantage to being a coward. Attack from behind and you don't have to look your victim in the eye.

"You didn't know anything about Michael, did you, Mr. Rodriguez? You didn't know that he would have graduated from college this year; that he majored in American history."

I look over at the Kydd, a fellow student of American history. He is watching Sally closely, shaking his head and swallowing hard. He is genuinely choked up.

"You didn't know that Michael was a member of the campus ROTC program, did you, Mr. Rodriguez? That's the Reserve Officers Training Corps. He hoped to become a Navy SEAL. He was wearing his U.S. Navy windbreaker the night you murdered him, but you probably didn't notice. Michael would have served his country well, Mr. Rodriguez, if you hadn't taken him from us."

Sally steps closer to Rodriguez, daring him to meet her eyes. He doesn't.

"You didn't know that Michael was slated to cocaptain the baseball team this year, did you, Mr. Rodriguez? You didn't know that he was on the dean's list, that he planned to pursue a master's degree in secondary education, that he dreamed of returning to his own small high school in Connecticut after completing his military career. He wanted to teach history there. He wanted to organize a debate team, coach the baseball team. You didn't know any of that, did you?"

I jump a little when Sally moves even closer to Rodriguez. The Kydd puts a steady hand on my arm. Sally points toward a young woman who is seated with Mr. Scott and the boys. The young woman has delicate features; her cheeks are soaked.

"You didn't know he was wild about his college sweetheart, did you, Mr. Rodriguez? You didn't know he was saving his money—the money you murdered him for—to buy her a ring. You didn't know he planned to give it to her this past Christmas.

"And you didn't know what a fine human being Michael was, did you, Mr. Rodriguez? You didn't know that he played baseball with his younger brothers and their friends whenever he was home on break. You didn't know that he spent hours helping his dad with projects around the house. You didn't know that he sent me a single yellow rose every year on my birthday.

"You didn't know that Michael was a funny person, did you, Mr. Rodriguez? That he loved animals. That he secretly listened to country music, and sang along when he thought no one could hear."

The Kydd laughs quietly at this. I look over at him again; there are tears in his eyes.

Sally continues. "You didn't know that Michael was a peacemaker, did you, Mr. Rodriguez? That he hated confrontation. That he always settled the disputes that arose between his younger brothers. That he always told them never to forget they are each other's best friends.

"But I know all of these things about Michael, Mr. Rodriguez. And because I know these things, I know what he wants me to do right now.

"You see, Mr. Rodriguez, Michael is at peace now. We are the ones who are tormented, the ones who love Michael, the ones who are left behind. We are tormented by what you did to him, by what you took from us.

"When Michael's heart stopped beating, my heart broke in two, Mr. Rodriguez. And it will never heal. Like you, I will serve a life sentence.

"In life, Michael never harbored a grudge. He was quick to understand and quick to forgive. I pay tribute to him now, by emulating him as best I can.

"I will never understand, Mr. Rodriguez. I will never understand why you did what you did. But—in honor of Michael—I forgive. I forgive you. And I pray that God will forgive you as well."

Forgiveness is more than Manuel Rodriguez can bear. He looks like a wild animal as he rears up on his shackled feet. I jump up too, and instinctively I reach for the Lady Smith. Rodriguez is too close to Sally Scott, shackled or not. The Kydd stiffens beside me when he sees my finger on the trigger.

Rodriguez screams into Sally's terrified face. "I didn't kill your kid, lady. I didn't kill him. I took his goddamned money. I took his watch. But I didn't kill him."

The court officers form a tight circle around Rodriguez and begin dragging him toward the side door. Sally moves deftly out of their path. I drop the Lady Smith back into my pocket. The Kydd exhales.

Rodriguez pokes his head and neck out between two guards. He juts his chin toward the other Scott boys but keeps his eyes focused on Sally. He is a savage.

"Better keep an eye on them, missus. Whoever killed your kid is still out there. So you better keep an eye on the two you got left. He's still out there, missu—"

Taking a signal from Judge Carroll, the guards gag Rodriguez, causing his words to come to an unnatural halt. In the Commonwealth of Massachusetts, Criminal Procedure Rule 45 gives the trial judge authority to remove a disruptive defendant from the courtroom at any time during the proceedings. The rule specifically authorizes gagging the defendant if the trial judge believes that's necessary to maintain order. Constitutional challenges to the rule have consistently failed.

Rodriguez is gone. The room is silent. Sally faces Judge Carroll, hugging the photograph of Michael. She's not crying yet, but she is beginning to shake. She looks up at the judge and sighs. "Lock him up, Your Honor. Please. Lock him up."

Sally returns to her seat. Judge Carroll turns toward Harry but doesn't look at him. Instead, the judge fusses with papers on his bench as he speaks. "Mr. Madigan, in light of your client's inability to control himself, which he's demonstrated twice now, I intend to sentence him in his absence. If you wish to say anything on his behalf, even though he's not present to hear it, you may do so now."

Harry stands, crosses the room, and hands me a new document. The Kydd leans over my shoulder to read. It's a Notice of Appeal. Harry is asking for a new trial for Rodriguez, and his request is based on two separate issues.

First, Harry challenges Judge Carroll's refusal to send the jurors back to their hotel rooms on the night of May 30, before the all-nighter that resulted in the verdict. Second, Harry challenges Judge Carroll's denial of the motion to set aside the verdict. In support of his argument on the second issue, Harry includes the photographs of the torsos of Michael Scott and Skippy Eldridge. And the whole package is copied to Woody Timmons at the *Cape Cod Times*.

This petition will go initially to a single justice of the Court of Appeals. If that justice believes Judge Carroll committed an error of law in making either of these rulings, he will recommend that the matter be reviewed by the full appellate panel.

Harry walks to the front of the courtroom and hands the same

Notice of Appeal to Judge Carroll. He stands like a statue in front of the judge and looks him squarely in the eyes. He doesn't speak until the silence in the room is deafening. "I've got nothing to say in this courtroom, Judge. Nothing."

When Harry turns back toward the defense table, his expression says it all. He just burned a bridge, and he knows it.

CHAPTER 28

Wednesday, June 9

Cedar Junction is one of only two maximum security prisons in the Commonwealth of Massachusetts. It's a massive and forbidding place, housing 850 inmates, all male. For the past thirty-six hours, Manuel Rodriguez has been one of them.

The penitentiary was originally named Walpole, after the town that is stuck with it. The citizens of Walpole grew tired of having their hometown confused with a maximum security prison and in the mid 1980s they petitioned for a change of the prison's name. As a result, the Commonwealth's legislature renamed the facility Cedar Junction, after an old railroad station in the town.

The locals might have been better served by changing the name of their town. To this day, everyone I know still refers to the prison as Walpole.

Walpole was built in 1955 and opened less than a year later. Its original perimeter is still in place, a concrete wall with eight observation towers. The wall is twenty feet high, with four strands of electri-

121

fied barbed wire stretched taut across the top. A few years ago, a new unit was added to the prison, and a ninth tower was added to the wall. Each tower is manned twenty-four hours a day by multiple guards with automatic weapons. The exact number is deliberately unspecified.

Harry came here yesterday and met with Rodriguez about his sentence, his pending appeal, and the new assault charges I filed against him. Rodriguez gave Harry a single piece of information, something he'd never told Harry before. It's something I should hear, Harry told me, something I should hear from Rodriguez firsthand. Harry says it's important, and that's good enough for me.

It took over an hour to drive here from Harry's office in Barnstable. The Kydd is covering for me at the office. I warned him that Geraldine will be furious with both of us when she finds out where I've gone. He agreed to cover for me anyway.

Harry rolls down the driver's side window of his beat-up old Jeep Wrangler and hands both his license and mine to the guard at the gate. The guard studies them carefully, comparing Harry with his license photo, then comparing me with mine.

"She's much better looking in person," Harry tells him.

The guard doesn't even let on he heard, but I turn bright red anyway, and Harry smiles at me. The uniform walks around the Wrangler looking in the windows. He takes notes on a clipboard, then stands behind the Jeep copying its plate number. Finally, he checks our names against the list of appointments approved by the superintendent.

"It's good to have friends in high places," Harry says.

The guard frowns, but just barely. He keeps our licenses and waves us through the gate. A second guard directs us to a predetermined parking spot. He takes Harry's keys, tags them, and slides a corresponding tag under the driver's side windshield wiper. He drops

Harry's keys into a cloth sack hanging from his belt, and points us toward a concrete walkway that leads to the front entrance.

The uniform at the gate must have notified the front desk of our arrival; the huge steel doors open as we approach them. A half dozen security cameras are rolling. Once inside, we are directed to put all of our possessions into a numbered plastic bin with a padlock. We are to take nothing past the front desk, we are told, but the clothes on our backs.

Harry raises his eyebrows and lets out a low whistle when I drop the Lady Smith into the plastic bin along with my cell phone. "Sweet Jesus, she's packing heat," he says.

A brusque, burly guard asks if I am wearing a wig. If so, he says, he will need to inspect it. Harry tugs on my hair to demonstrate its authenticity. The burly guard is not amused.

"What about you, sir, are you wearing a toupee?"

Harry is delighted by the question. He grins broadly and tugs at his own thick tangle as he responds. "No, sir. This is the real McCoy."

The burly guard remains visibly unimpressed. He directs us through the metal detector, and walks a short distance from us to converse with a guard who looks like a younger version of himself.

While we wait, I take in the details of the cavernous lobby. Three separate visitors' dress codes are posted. They cover an entire wall. The first code is just for men and lists dozens of restrictions. No denim. No black, navy blue, or gray sweatshirts. No blue chambray shirts. The code for women is even longer. No leotards. No gym shorts. No nylons. The third code applies to everyone. Just one pair of earrings. Just one religious medal. Underpants required.

The younger guard tells us to follow him. He leads us down a narrow hallway, past a series of numbered doors. When we reach the last one, number twelve, he selects a key from the ring on his belt loop and opens it. He steps back to allow us to enter, and follows us inside.

Every inmate at Walpole is classified as a serious flight risk and a grave physical threat to himself, the other inmates, and the prison staff. Every inmate here is confined to his cell at all times, except when he is removed for reasons preapproved by the prison hierarchy. On those occasions, the prisoner leaves his cell under armed escort and in restraints. That is how Manuel Rodriguez arrives in the cubicle adjacent to the small space where Harry and I are waiting.

The space is too tiny to be called a room. The ceiling is low— Harry has only about an inch of headroom—and there are no furnishings, not even a chair. Three of the four walls are made of whitewashed cement block. The fourth is two-thirds cement block, the top third bulletproof glass. Microphones and speakers on each side of the glass allow communication between one side of the wall and the other.

Harry looks first at the two guards with Rodriguez, then at the guard who stands behind us. "Gentlemen, you'll excuse us? This conference is protected by the attorney-client privilege. Your superintendent has approved it."

One of the guards with Rodriguez looks confused. He probably has seen both Harry and me on the television news. He knows I don't represent Rodriguez. But Harry holds up the written authorization, signed by the superintendent, and the guard's questioning look disappears. All three guards exit, in blind submission to the institutional chain of command. They take up posts outside the doors.

Harry doesn't waste a second. "Manny, this is important. This might help you. You need to tell Attorney Nickerson what you told me yesterday. All of it."

Rodriguez turns slowly toward me, his upper lip curled, daggers emanating from his eyes. Then he turns, just as slowly, back to Harry. "What's she gonna do, let me go home?"

Harry presses his fists against the glass. "Look, we went through this yesterday. This is your only shot at setting things straight. Maybe it's a lousy shot. But it's the only one you've got left, pal. Take it now or leave it for good."

Rodriguez is unmoved. "So what do you want me to tell her?"

Harry is losing patience. He enunciates each word carefully. "Tell her where you were and what you did Memorial Day a year ago, during the predawn hours. And tell her all of it."

Rodriguez looks back at me. "I was in Orleans," he says.

Minutes pass. Rodriguez says nothing more. I can't believe Harry brought me here for this. "You expect me to believe him?" I ask Harry. "You expect me to think that two different witnesses lied about seeing him at Chatham Light, and he's all of a sudden telling the truth?"

Harry doesn't look at me. His eyes are boring into Rodriguez. "Goddammit, tell her."

"I was in Orleans first, then I went to Chatham."

"So what?" I ask him.

Harry pounds on the glass. "Tell her what you did in Orleans, and tell her now."

Rodriguez puts his face close to the glass and stares at me. Only when my eyes are glued to his does he speak again. "I killed a guy."

I don't know what I was expecting, but I know it wasn't this.

Rodriguez is laughing at me now, enjoying his control over the situation. "I killed the guy at the Orleans Pit Stop. He wouldn't open the cash box, and he set off some goddamned alarm, man, so I shot him." He pauses to make sure I am still looking into his eyes; he's directing this show. "Right in the head."

My blood runs cold and Rodriguez laughs again. "I couldn't get the damn thing open, man, and the cops were coming, so I split. The sirens came from the north, so I went south, man, out of Orleans, through East Harwich and into Chatham. I stopped at the lighthouse and went down to the beach to throw my piece in the ocean."

I don't know why he's telling me this. But he keeps talking. "That guy—the one you're all worked up about—he was already dead, man. He was sprawled on the beach when I got there." Again, Rodriguez peers deep into my eyes. "But he wasn't cold yet."

This fact apparently strikes Rodriguez as funny; he laughs yet again. "I checked him for money, and I took what I found. I took his watch, too. I was countin' on some cash from the Pit Stop, man. I had some people I needed to pay."

None of this makes sense. I can't think clearly. I turn to Harry, but he's still staring holes through Rodriguez. I look back at Rodriguez too, and he is waiting for me. He narrows his eyes and hisses, "So I know what you did with the shirt, lady."

"The shirt?"

His entire upper lip curls back. He's missing three teeth, and the ones he has left are yellow and brown. He looks like a rabid animal.

"Yeah, the shirt. I wasn't wearing no goddamned flannel shirt. I didn't even keep my tee shirt on for long. I was sweatin' like a pig, man. That flannel shirt was in my trunk for months. If that guy's blood was on it, lady, you put it there."

My head is spinning. Rodriguez is still talking. Now that he's started, he can't seem to stop.

"So you think you put some totally innocent slob in the slammer. You get off on that, I guess. You think you're real smart. But you ain't very smart after all. You thought you framed an innocent guy, but it turns out you just framed me. And I did kill a guy, just not the guy you said."

Rodriguez moves back from the glass and spits on the floor. His shackles allow only a baby step, and he almost topples backward, but it doesn't faze him.

"It don't make no difference to me, man. But it might make a difference to that good-lookin' lady with the red hair. I got kids too, ya know. I got feelings. I feel sorry for that lady. Whoever killed her kid ain't in the slammer. He's out there lookin' around."

Harry bangs on the door and all three guards reappear instantly. "We're finished here," Harry tells them.

Rodriguez disagrees. "Hey, man, I ain't finished. I never said I was finished."

"You're finished," Harry tells him.

The guards move Rodriguez out the door like a piece of furniture.

"Hey, Madigan, thanks for nothin'. The only thing you ever done for me was knock me out. Thanks a lot, man."

The heavy metal door slams shut.

"Harry," I start. But he stops me.

"Let's talk outside," he says, nodding toward our escort.

"But Harry . . ."

"I know," he says.

I can't stop myself. "Harry, that's the Buckley case. Jim Buckley was the clerk who got shot in Orleans that night. He didn't die. He survived."

"I know, Marty. We're going to see him next."

CHAPTER 29

Jim Buckley retired from the Commonwealth Electric Company after thirty-five years of service. Three months later, he went looking for a job. His wife insisted, he later told the Orleans detectives. He was driving her crazy.

Jim found a job at the Orleans Pit Stop, an old-fashioned, full-service general store. He worked from six in the evening until two in the morning, five days a week, until Memorial Day a year ago. On that day, just before closing time, a man who had entered the store like an ordinary customer suddenly brandished a firearm and demanded the contents of the cash register. Jim Buckley tripped the alarm and tried to escape through a side door. The gunman fired a single shot into the back of his head.

Paramedics rushed Jim Buckley to Cape Cod Hospital in Hyannis. Once stabilized, he was airlifted to Massachusetts General Hospital in Boston and taken straight into surgery. Six hours later, surgeons reattached the back of his skull and closed the surgical field, the bullet still lodged in its original resting place. It was too close to the brain stem, they said, to be removed.

Geraldine lives in Orleans. She takes every unsolved violent crime in her hometown as a personal affront. Jim Buckley's case is no exception. She has been hounding the Orleans Police Department since the day it happened, to no avail. They've had no leads. No prints were left at the scene. No gun was ever found.

It was months before Jim Buckley was able to communicate with the Orleans investigators. He described his assailant as either a light-skinned black man or a dark-skinned Latino; average height, average weight. Wearing faded dungarees and a plain white tee shirt. No distinguishing characteristics, so far as Jim could recall.

It's two o'clock by the time Harry and I approach the Sagamore Bridge, heading back to Cape Cod. It will take another forty minutes to reach Jim Buckley's house in Orleans. It's clear that I won't make it into the office at all today. I called the Kydd to tell him so as soon as we left Walpole. He's got me covered, he said.

Harry hasn't said much since we left the prison. Like me, he is probably trying to sort out the ramifications of this new piece of information. I shift in my seat and face his rugged profile as he drives across the bridge. "You know, Harry, Rodriguez could be duping us both. The Buckley attack got plenty of press coverage. Rodriguez might be well aware of the fact that Buckley survived that shooting. If he knows that, he's got good reason to want to trade the attack on Michael Scott for the attack on Buckley. At least he'd have the possibility of parole on the horizon."

"I've thought of that, Marty. Rodriguez is no dope, that's for sure. He's capable of putting on a convincing act. If Buckley can't identify him, we'll have to assume that's a real possibility."

Silence settles on us again. We are entering Orleans when I verbalize the question that I think has been plaguing both of us. "What if Buckley does identify Rodriguez? What then, Harry?"

Harry sighs and turns down a side street into a tree-lined residential area. "Then we have to face some ugly facts, Marty."

I shift in my seat again and stare out the window. I've about had my fill of ugly facts for now. But Harry keeps talking. "Fact number one, Rodriguez is in jail for the wrong crime, serving the wrong sentence. Fact number two, whoever killed the Scott kid was still on the streets when Eldridge was murdered. Fact number three, he's still out there."

Harry stops the Jeep in the middle of the road and stares at me. I know what he's going to say next. "Fact number four is the worst one of all, Marty. If Rodriguez didn't kill the Scott kid, then somebody went to great lengths to make it look like he did."

I am having trouble absorbing this. My mind is racing to find an alternate explanation. "What if Rodriguez did both? What if he shot Jim Buckley and then killed Michael Scott?"

My question sounds ridiculous even to me.

Harry pulls into the driveway next to a well-maintained shingled ranch with a freshly cut lawn. "Think about it, Marty. Rodriguez shoots Buckley, then drives to Lighthouse Beach to get rid of the weapon. He sees the Scott kid and decides to do him too. And he uses a knife? He's got a gun in his hands and he uses a knife instead?"

Harry is right, of course, but I'm not ready to say so. We get out of the car in silence.

Jim Buckley is waving to us from his back porch. He shakes our hands as if we are old friends, and leads us into a small, tidy kitchen where his wife is waiting, a grandmotherly lady wearing a pink apron. The Buckleys are the picture of working-class, retired America. Framed photographs of their adult children and grandchildren are on every available shelf. We sit down at a mottled red kitchen table with stainless steel legs, and Mrs. Buckley brings iced tea.

Harry gets straight to the point. "Mr. Buckley, thanks for meeting with us on such short notice. This will only take a few minutes, I promise."

Jim Buckley waves his hands in the air as if he's got all the time in the world. Harry unzips a leather case he brought from the Jeep and takes out a single poster board. On it are twelve mug shots.

There are strict rules governing the procedures to be used when a crime victim—or any witness, for that matter—is asked to identify an attacker from an array of photographs. If the rules are not followed, the identification will not be admitted at trial. Worse yet, if the court finds that the photographic display was too suggestive, the witness's testimony may be deemed tainted, and excluded altogether.

Harry's photographic display passes all of the tests. There are a dozen photographs of men in their mid-to-late twenties. Four are light-skinned black men. Four are dark-skinned Latinos. Four are Hispanic. Only one is Rodriguez.

Jim Buckley breaks down as soon as Harry lays the board on the red kitchen table. "You've got him. By God, you've got him."

He points straight to Rodriguez and takes off his glasses as he looks from Harry to me, shaking his head. He wipes tears from his eyes. "After all this time. By God, you've finally got him."

CHAPTER 30

Thursday, June 10

"You went to Walpole? With Madigan? I'm surprised they let you in. I'm even more surprised they let him out. Is there something wrong with you, Martha?"

As usual, Rob and I are seated at his desk and Geraldine is towering over us, pacing and chain-smoking. I had wanted to speak with Rob alone about the Rodriguez confession and the Buckley identification, but that proved impossible. Geraldine knew something was up as soon as she looked at me this morning. I am lousy with secrets.

"Geraldine, Harry came to me saying he had just been given important information for the first time. I was the prosecutor on the case. I had a duty to go hear it for myself."

"A duty? To Rodriguez? You think you had a duty to listen to Rodriguez cop to a lesser offense now that he's convicted of murder one? You think there's a single inmate at Walpole who wouldn't like to cop to a lesser offense? Do you have a duty to listen to all of them?"

I'm actually a couple of inches taller than Geraldine, but it never feels that way. I am tired of her looking down at me, so I get to my feet before I answer. "My duty is to the integrity of the system."

Geraldine tosses her head back and blows smoke at the ceiling. She gives me a sidelong glance, a look that says even I can't be naive enough to mean what I just said.

"Look, Geraldine, I didn't believe him. Not at first. But when Jim Buckley was so certain, I felt I had to bring the confession and the identification to Rob's attention."

"Why, Martha? To undermine the conviction on the Scott murder? To play into your harebrained theory about numbered corpses? Is that why?"

Rob walks around his desk and stops short on the other side of Geraldine, waving one hand in the air to silence her. This is a rare move on his part. "Geraldine, Marty is right. We have a positive I.D. from the survivor of an attempted homicide. And like it or not, we have a confession—real or fictitious—from the man who's been identified as the shooter. We have an absolute duty to investigate further. You know that as well as I do. I suggest you set up a time to meet with Jim Buckley yourself. If he's as sure as Marty says he is, then we've got to pursue this."

Geraldine is surprised, to say the least, and with good reason. Rob hasn't issued a directive to Geraldine since *Commonwealth versus Lucas*. That calamity ended almost nine years ago, but Geraldine won't let the memory fade. Not a week goes by that she doesn't find some reason to mention Collette Lucas's name. And Rob still flinches every time she does.

I had been with the office little more than a year when thirty-two-year-old Collette Lucas stood trial for the first-degree murder of her fifty-year-old husband, Warren. Geraldine tried the case and I watched every minute I could. Because of the nature of the accusation, so did most of New England. Collette Lucas murdered her husband, Geraldine charged, by dropping a generous handful of amphetamines into his highball, his fourth of the evening. Collette Lucas's motive was simple: greed.

Warren Lucas suffered from advanced heart disease and had undergone double-bypass surgery little more than a year before his death. His demise was originally attributed to natural causes. But when out-of-town relatives traveled to the Barnstable County District Attorney's office crying foul play, Geraldine concluded they were on to something.

Collette Lucas, it turned out, stood to inherit all of her husband's worldly possessions. His estate was modest; it included only their small Cape Cod cottage and about ten thousand dollars in liquid assets. But to Collette Lucas, Geraldine argued, the combination amounted to a veritable fortune.

Herb Wilkins, now retired but then a well-respected criminal defense lawyer, was appointed by the court to defend Collette Lucas. Harry Madigan, already ten years into his career at the Public Defender's office, was assigned to protect the interests of Collette Lucas's sixteen-year-old son, Dylan Jackson.

Dylan Jackson was the product of Collette's teen pregnancy. When the teenaged father disappeared, Collette was forced to abort her education halfway through the tenth grade. Four years later, Collette Jackson and Warren Lucas set up housekeeping. They married the following summer.

Dylan Jackson was present in the home at the time of the alleged amphetamine poisoning. Geraldine believed he assisted his mother in moving his stepfather's large body from the dinner table to the living room couch, thereby minimizing any connection between his death and the recently drained highball. Collette Lucas, Geraldine contended, was far too small to have moved her overweight husband alone. Though Dylan was not then accused of any crime, he was at least technically vulnerable to being charged as an accessory after the fact.

Geraldine succeeded in obtaining a court order directing that Warren Lucas's body be exhumed in order to revisit the cause-of-death determination. The body had been embalmed, of course, but at trial Geraldine's toxicologist testified that he was able to isolate a small amount of body fluid not contaminated by the embalming agents. That sample, he said, tested positive for amphetamines. The amphetamine level in the sample, he testified, indicated that Mr. Lucas had ingested an exceedingly high dose of the drugs just prior to his death.

The Commonwealth's pathologist testified that Warren Lucas's remaining natural coronary arteries were almost entirely blocked, but the two bypass arteries were clear and functioning. There was no anatomical explanation, he said, for the trauma the heart had suffered.

Next, the Commonwealth's expert cardiologist elaborated on the properties of amphetamines. The drugs stimulate the central nervous system, he explained. A dose of the size ingested by Mr. Lucas would send the system into overdrive, forcing the heart to work harder and harder, eventually beyond its limits. Warren Lucas's death, the doctor opined, was caused by a combination of acute amphetamine poisoning and heart disease. Neither factor alone would have killed him.

Repeatedly during the months leading up to trial Geraldine tried to interview Dylan Jackson. Harry refused. He would not allow Dylan to answer any questions, he told Geraldine. Not before the trial, and not during it. If Geraldine subpoenaed the boy to testify, Harry promised, he would instruct his client to take the Fifth. And that's exactly what he did.

Geraldine called Dylan Jackson to the stand after all the expert testimony was in. Harry allowed him to state his name and address for the record, and that was it. In response to every question that followed, sixteen-year-old Dylan recited the litany Harry had taught him. "Relying upon the advice of counsel, I decline to answer the question posed, on the grounds that the content of my answer might incriminate me."

It was at this point in the trial that Rob intervened. He had been watching from the sidelines, but joined Geraldine at the counsel table to suggest that she offer immunity to Dylan Jackson in exchange for his testimony. The boy's answers were critical, Rob said, to make the factual case against his mother. Without his testimony, the jury might well conclude that Warren Lucas took the popular street drugs voluntarily. And Rob had no interest in pursuing the accessory charge anyway.

Geraldine resisted. She told Rob she could make the factual case through Tyrone Briggs, the teenager who said he sold the amphetamines to Collette Lucas. In exchange for leniency in several drug-related charges pending against him, Briggs was prepared to testify that Collette Lucas told him she intended to use the drugs to kill her husband. Briggs claimed Collette told him she knew the drugs would be deadly, given her husband's already compromised heart. That would be enough, Geraldine said, to enable the jury to convict. She didn't need Dylan Jackson's testimony. Besides, there was something about the boy that made Geraldine uneasy.

Rob was uncomfortable with allowing the Commonwealth's case to hinge on the jury's evaluation of Tyrone Briggs. The defense lawyers would parade every detail of his plea agreement before the panel and, after that, Rob said, Tyrone's credibility would be just about nil. But Geraldine persisted. She did not want to proceed with Dylan Jackson.

In the end, Rob prevailed. The trial judge called a one-hour recess, during which Rob, Geraldine, and Harry hammered out the terms of the immunity agreement in a courthouse conference room. The deal was hurriedly put in writing and approved by the court.

When Dylan Jackson returned to the witness stand, he was cloaked with immunity from prosecution for any misdeed associated in any way with his stepfather's death. And his immunity was absolute; Harry wouldn't settle for anything less.

Geraldine moved for permission to treat Dylan Jackson as a hostile witness and the court allowed it. That meant Geraldine could conduct her direct examination of Dylan as if it were a cross-examination. Geraldine asked questions that called for yes or no answers. The boy was obligated to respond accordingly.

But Dylan's yes or no answers didn't make any sense. Not one of them fit Geraldine's theory of the case. Exasperated, Geraldine ultimately committed the cardinal sin of trial practice. She asked a hostile witness an open-ended question. "We know there were massive amounts of amphetamines in your stepfather's system," she blurted out. "Did it get there by magic?" She rued those words even before Dylan answered.

Dylan Jackson told the court, in a firm, calm voice, that it was he who dropped the handful of amphetamines in his stepfather's highball. His mother, he said, was in no condition to do so.

Dylan explained that his stepfather had been beating his mother for as long as he could remember. The abuse was almost never severe enough to force her to seek medical attention, but it often sent her to bed bloodied. And it always left her in tears.

Dylan went on to tell a silent—and stunned—courtroom that he had stood by helplessly for too many years. He had watched his mother bleed—and cry—too many times. Since his mother seemed unable to leave her abusive husband, Dylan decided his stepfather should leave—for good.

To this day, Geraldine maintains that Dylan Jackson fabricated his tale, and that Collette Lucas got away with murder. I watched that teenager testify, and I don't agree with Geraldine. But Rob does. He hasn't challenged Geraldine's instincts since. Until now.

Geraldine takes it in stride, though, I'll give her that. "All right," she says. "All right. For Christ's sake, I'll talk to Jim Buckley." She pauses for a long drag on her cigarette, shakes her head at me, and lets out a short laugh as she exhales. "Forget Walpole, Martha. We ought to send you up to Bridgewater. Find out why you've taken leave of your senses."

I laugh too. It's funny she should say that. If only she knew.

CHAPTER 31

Friday, June 11

The Massachusetts Correctional Institution at Bridgewater—commonly called Bridgewater State Hospital—houses the Commonwealth's criminally insane men. It is the only maximum security forensic hospital in Massachusetts. It has three hundred beds. For the past ten days Eddie Malone has been in one of them.

Every patient admitted to Bridgewater State Hospital is either charged with a crime or convicted of one. The offenses include the worst of felonies. Like Eddie Malone, every patient here is initially the subject of a court-ordered psychiatric evaluation. The length of the observation period is governed by statute and can range from twenty to forty days, depending upon the purpose of the evaluation. At the end of the observation period, the patient may be recommitted for a longer term if the court finds that he needs further treatment or evaluation.

The patients are segregated according to the severity of their afflictions and the heinousness of their crimes. Eddie Malone is housed with the worst of them.

All units at Bridgewater State Hospital are locked, but on Eddie's unit, each room is locked as well. There are twenty beds on this ward, and at least that many armed guards. The hospital administrator who led Harry and me here consults with one of them before taking her leave without so much as a backward glance at us. The guard takes over, leading us down a brightly lit hall toward a small conference room. Harry made advance arrangements for us to meet privately with Eddie Malone.

The area that would be known as the nurses' station in an ordinary hospital is more like a command center here. Twenty closed-circuit monitors line the counter, each providing a view of the interior of one patient room. As we pass, I scan the screens looking for Eddie Malone. I feel a sudden need to know how horrific this has been for him.

Some of the patients are bound at the wrists and ankles and cuffed to their beds. Some are similarly bound but cuffed to their chairs. Two are in straitjackets. When I finally spot Eddie Malone, I see that he is not physically bound or restrained in any way. I feel an odd sense of relief.

All patients are restrained, though, when they are removed from the confines of their rooms. No exceptions. Eddie Malone is cuffed and shackled when the armed guard delivers him to the conference room. Eddie turns his back to Harry and shakes hands with him from behind, the only way he can in cuffs. He gives me a slight, gentlemanly bow before he sits down across the small Formica table from me.

In some ways, Eddie Malone looks better than I would have thought possible. He is clean shaven and his eyes are clear. He looks well rested and well fed. Three square meals a day and no booze have made a noticeable difference already.

But his spirit is sapped. I see that at once. When I look across the table at Eddie Malone, I see no sign of the sassy little man who pro-claimed his innocence so doggedly in Judge Gould's courtroom. Instead, this new, watered-down version of Eddie Malone sits quietly, meekly even, waiting for whatever is going to happen to him next.

Harry claps him on the back. "You okay, Eddie?"

"Sure, Mr. Madigan. I'm just fine."

"Okay. Then let's do exactly what we talked about yesterday, Eddie. I'm going to ask you to tell Attorney Nickerson everything you can remember about Memorial Day. All right?"

"You goin' to help me?"

"Sure I will. I'll ask you the questions. You tell Attorney Nicker-son the answers. If you don't remember, just say so."

"All right, then." Eddie looks over at me and tries to smile, but he looks like a schoolboy about to take final exams.

"Where did you spend the night before Memorial Day, Eddie?"

"At the Nor'easter."

The Nor'easter is a watering hole frequented year-round by the rough and tumble among Chatham locals. It's just down the road from Harding's Beach.

"What time did you leave?"

"Closing time, I reckon."

"And where did you go, Eddie, when you left the Nor'easter?"

"I went to Harding's Beach."

"Do you remember going to Harding's Beach?"

"Nope."

"Then how do you know you went there?"

"'Cause I woke up there the next day, that's how."

"And how did you wake up the next day, Eddie?"

Eddie looks at me and swallows hard. "Well, I heard screamin'. I jumped up when I heard it. There was a lady and a man there. When they saw me, they started screamin' louder. Hollerin' all over the place, they were. So I figured I better get out of there."

"Where did you go, Eddie?"

"I went to Shirley's. Figured I'd get some breakfast and some coffee."

Shirley's Diner is just across the road from the Nor'easter. It opens at four o'clock each morning, catering to the commercial fishing fleet.

"And what did you do next, Eddie?"

"Well, while I was eatin', Ricky Sparrow come in askin' does anybody want to go codfishin'. Just a day trip. The guy that usually fishes with him dint show up."

"And you volunteered?"

"Yeah, and nobody else did. He wouldn'ta taken me if he coulda taken somebody else. Ricky don't like me much."

"So you spent the day offshore, fishing with Ricky Sparrow?"

"Yeah. Made some decent money, too."

"And what time did you get back to Chatham?"

"I don't know. After dark."

I am losing interest. Eddie has already told me he was at the crime scene and doesn't remember how he got there. What he did later in the day really doesn't matter. But Harry pushes on.

"Where did you go next, Eddie?"

"I went back to the Nor'easter."

"Did you sit at the bar?"

"Yup. I always sit at the bar."

"Eddie, who was the bartender?"

I feel a sudden rush of adrenaline. These questions are irrelevant. Harry doesn't ask irrelevant questions—ever. I am missing something. Harry sees something here that I don't. I sit up in my chair and inject myself into this question-and-answer session. "The bartender? What difference does that make?"

Harry stays focused on Eddie. "It matters, Eddie. Try to remember."

"Oh, I remember. It was Laurie Griffin. But don't you go draggin' her into this, Mr. Madigan. She's the nicest lady on Cape Cod."

Harry laughs. "She is a nice lady, Eddie. And I've been real nice to her. I swear."

I wonder when Harry had occasion to be nice to Laurie Griffin. He continues. "Did you use the rest room while you were at the Nor'easter, Eddie?"

Eddie chuckles. Even he realizes how far afield the questioning has gone.

"I reckon I did, Mr. Madigan. I was there a long time—drinkin' beer and all—I reckon I did."

Harry nods. "What time did you leave the Nor'easter, Eddie?"

"Closing time, I reckon."

"And where did you go?"

Eddie chuckles again and shakes his head, as if even he can't believe the answer he is about to give. "I went back to Harding's Beach. I must be stupid or somethin'."

"Do you remember going there, Eddie?"

"I do, Mr. Madigan. I remember hopin' those screamin' people would be gone when I got there."

"And were they gone, Eddie?"

"Oh, they was gone, all right."

"So what did you do?"

"I went to sleep. I got a spot there—right between two sand dunes—it's protected from the wind. It gets cold at night with that wind, even in the summertime."

"Then what?"

"Well, next thing I know, my hands is cuffed behind my back, and some kid in a uniform—looks like he ain't old enough to shave yet—

he's readin' me my rights. The whole parkin' lot's full of cruisers with their lights flashin'. They even had a couple of state cars there. You'da thought I was Bonnie and Clyde both, if you'd seen it."

Eddie Malone looks at me with his clear, defeated eyes. "You know the rest, ma'am."

One look at Harry tells me I don't know the rest. Not even close.

CHAPTER 32

Harry pulls into the first truck stop we see after leaving Bridgewater State Hospital. "Lunch," he announces, and winks at me as he grabs his briefcase from the backseat.

Food doesn't interest me at the moment, but Harry's explanation for his questioning does. I follow him across the large parking lot. It's so hot here that the blacktop is melting, and it sticks to the bottoms of my shoes. I see it clinging to the bottoms of Harry's shoes too, but he doesn't seem to notice. Geraldine will undoubtedly bring it to his attention next time she sees him.

It's obvious that Harry has been here before. He maneuvers his way around the gas pumps and the eighteen-wheelers and heads straight toward the neon EAT sign over the front door. He holds it open for me, and bows as if he is the maitre d', though I doubt that this particular establishment has one. At least it's air-conditioned.

The place is a genuine, old-fashioned diner, complete with a juke-box in every booth. A hand-printed sign at the entrance tells us to seat ourselves. Harry chooses a booth at the far end of the room, a good distance from the other patrons. I slide onto a red vinyl bench across the table from him and wait while he reads the daily specials with an urgency that suggests he hasn't eaten for a week.

He's a good man, Harry Madigan. The depth of his compassion for Eddie Malone is admirable; compassion is a tough trait to hang on to in this business. I've grown fond of Harry in a way I never expected. It must be the rumpled suits.

Two young men seated on the other side of the room have a pile of quarters in the middle of their table. They feed the hungry jukebox at regular intervals, and the woeful lyrics of jilted cowboys fill the diner. I can't help but think of what Sally Scott said about her son and country lyrics. If Michael Scott were here, I guess he would secretly sing along.

Harry pushes the paper placemats and silverware to the far end of the table and opens his briefcase in the middle. A large waitress with orange hair tied up in a bun appears at our table with a coffee pot. She turns our mugs over and pours, casting a disapproving frown at the piled silverware and crumpled placemats.

"He did it," I tell her, pointing an accusing finger at Harry.

Harry stares at me in mock dismay, then smiles sheepishly at the orange-haired waitress. "It's temporary, I promise. I'll have it all fixed up before the food comes."

The waitress all but melts in the warmth of his smile. She takes our orders and wags her finger at Harry before she leaves, as if he were her favorite nephew who'd just been a little bit naughty. Harry is a pro. I can't help laughing at him.

As soon as the waitress leaves us, Harry takes three documents from his briefcase, closes it, and slides it under the table. He puts all three documents in front of me and resets his own placemat and silverware. Mine remain piled in the corner.

I examine the first page of each document. Each one is an affidavit. The first is from Shirley Donaldson, the owner of Shirley's Diner. The second is from Ricky Sparrow, the fisherman. And the third is from the nicest lady on Cape Cod, Laurie Griffin.

I skim the affidavits quickly. Each one confirms some portion of Eddie's account of his whereabouts on Memorial Day and the night before. Eddie was at the Nor'easter until two o'clock the morning of the holiday, the regular closing time. He was at Shirley's Diner from about five-fifteen until six, when he left with Ricky Sparrow.

Eddie fished with Sparrow all day on the holiday. It was dark when they got back to the Chatham Fish Pier. Eddie was back at the Nor'easter again that night. Upon his arrival, he bought a round of drinks for everyone at the bar. He stayed until closing at two the next morning.

It takes a few minutes for me to realize that the last paragraph of Shirley Donaldson's affidavit is identical to the last paragraph of Laurie Griffin's. Each woman testifies: "At no time did I observe any blood, dried or otherwise, anywhere on the person of Eddie Malone. Moreover, there were no bloodstains, or stains of any kind, on the floor near Eddie Malone's seat, in the men's room, or anywhere else in the establishment, after he left."

I flip to the last page of Ricky Sparrow's affidavit. His final paragraph opens with the same statement as the other two, but then it changes. ". . . The wind had been running against the tide and seas had been choppy most of the day. Spray from large waves broke regularly over the side of the boat. Eddie Malone didn't have any oilskins. He was drenched all day. If there were stains of any kind on his pant cuffs, socks, and sneakers when he boarded, they would have been gone by the time we got back."

The orange-haired waitress reappears with our food. She sets Harry's enormous platter in front of him, but holds my modest plate in the air, resting her free hand on her hip. Harry lifts the affidavits from the table, resets my placemat and silverware, and apologizes for me. "You'll have to excuse her," he says, as if I'm not here. "She doesn't get out much."

The waitress shakes her head, but she's smiling as she leaves. I roll my eyes at Harry, the way Luke so often rolls his at me, and point with my fork at the affidavits in his hand. "So what?" I ask him.

Harry is stunned. "What do you mean, so what?"

"So Eddie was smart enough not to wear bloody clothes in public. So what? He's not charged with being a moron."

"Marty, don't you see? Eddie wasn't arrested until the following morning."

My fork freezes in midair. Harry is right. I see it now, but Harry explains anyway. "Marty, if Eddie had ditched his bloody clothes after murdering Skippy Eldridge, he sure as hell wouldn't have put them back on later. And if he had worn his bloody clothes into town, surely somebody would have noticed. But if you want to believe that Shirley Donaldson somehow missed a guy walking around her diner with blood on his pants and sneakers, then the salt water would have washed it away. There wouldn't have been any blood on his pants and sneakers the next morning."

I lower my fork and sink back against the vinyl bench as the full weight of these facts bears down on me. Harry continues. "And if there really was blood on Eddie's pants and sneakers when he was arrested at three o'clock, why the hell didn't Laurie Griffin see any trace of it when Eddie left the bar at two o'clock?"

Harry puts his elbows on the table, leans forward until his face is almost touching mine, and lowers his voice to a whisper. "Marty," he says, "somebody is tampering with evidence."

CHAPTER 33

Sunday, June 13

For the first time ever, Luke is looking forward to his visit with Ralph. For the first time ever, Luke is ready to leave the house as soon as Ralph arrives. For the first time ever, I haven't had to explain why these visits with his father are necessary. I realize, of course, that Ralph is incidental. The Boston Red Sox get the credit. Still, I think, it's progress.

And I am grateful for the time I will have alone today. I plan to review every page of both the Scott file and the Eldridge file. Then I will prepare an outline of the facts that have surfaced during the past five days. Tomorrow I will present all of it to Rob. The Rodriguez confession; the Buckley identification; the affidavits from Laurie Griffin, Ricky Sparrow, and Shirley Donaldson. Rob doesn't have to believe in numbered corpses to see that something is wrong here.

Ralph pulls into the driveway at one o'clock. It will take a couple of hours to get to Fenway Park on a Sunday afternoon and, at Luke's urging, they are planning to get there two hours before game time to watch batting practice. Luke is hoping to snag a couple of autographs as well. He picked up a new baseball and a black felt-tipped pen just for that purpose.

Ralph knocks on the kitchen door and lets himself in when he sees me working at the old pine table. Danny Boy gets to his feet and gives Ralph his usual greeting. Ralph growls back at him. Luke is in the kitchen in a flash, and Ralph is obviously surprised.

"All set, Luke?" Ralph seems unusually upbeat. Maybe he's a closet baseball fan.

"You bet I am." Luke rubs Danny Boy's head, then gives me a kiss. The phrase "first things first" comes to mind.

"Bye, Mom. See you tonight."

"When tonight?" I direct the question to Ralph.

"I don't know," Ralph says absently. "Does it matter?"

Ah, the blissful nonchalance of the once-a-week parent.

"Well, there is school tomorrow," I remind him.

Ralph turns to Luke. "Aren't you guys out yet?"

"Not till Friday." Luke shakes his head sadly, as if the injustice of this fact is apparent to all.

Ralph looks back at me and shrugs. He's always had a hard time answering questions that call for concrete facts. "I don't know," he says. "How about midnight?"

"Midnight? On a school night? How about ten?"

"Marty, be reasonable . . ."

I hate it when he says that.

". . . The game will run a few hours. It will take a couple of hours to drive back here. And I thought we'd stop some place for dinner. How about eleven?"

Luke chimes in. "Come on, Mom."

This is a new feeling. Ralph and Luke on one side; me on the other.

"All right. Eleven. But no later."

I follow them out the kitchen door. Never one to be left behind, Danny Boy is on my heels. I wave at the back of the BMW, and Luke waves out the passenger-side window until they are out of sight.

Danny Boy stretches out on the deck and rests his chin on his front paws. I sit down in the warm sunshine on the step beside him and rub his ears, but he whimpers anyway. Maybe he knows something I don't.

CHAPTER 34

Monday, June 14

Classes at Chatham High School begin promptly at seven-thirty. The schedule works out well for Luke and me. I drop him at school at seven-fifteen or so, then head straight to work. Most days, I am at my desk before eight.

We're behind schedule this morning. I'm driving faster than usual, and that always brings a smile to Luke's lips. He holds an imaginary microphone up to his mouth and assumes the expression of a self-impressed news anchor. "Assistant District Attorney arrested," he intones, "for tearing up Morris Island Road."

Just before Chatham Light, Morris Island Road intersects with Bridge Street on the left. The Beach and Tennis Club, with its octet of oceanside courts, is on the right, the pounding surf of the Atlantic just beyond. I normally go straight here, past Chatham Light and down Main Street toward the high school. But this morning my attention is drawn to four Chatham squad cars, lights flashing, halfway down Bridge Street. The Town of Chatham owns only eight squad cars, and four of them are on Bridge Street. I automatically hit my left-turn signal.

"Mom, I'm going to be late."

"I'll give you a note, Luke. Something's going on here."

Sergeant Kathy Carmine steps into the road, ordering me to stop. I lean out the window and wave to her.

"Oh, sorry, Marty. I should have recognized the Thunderbird. You can go ahead, but . . ." She hesitates, and nods toward Luke. "It isn't pretty."

That's all I need to hear. "Luke, hop out."

"What?"

"Hop out. You wait here with Sergeant Carmine. I'll be right back."

Luke rolls his eyes at me as he opens the car door. "Mom, it's probably a car accident. I think I can handle it."

"You're probably right, Luke. Stay here. I'll be right back."

The Mitchell River Bridge gives Bridge Street its name. It's an old wooden drawbridge that spans the waters of Stage Harbor, and it's a favorite fishing spot for locals and tourists alike. The drawbridge still operates the old-fashioned way. When a vessel too large to clear it approaches, Chatham's Chief of Police is summoned to open it.

The Chief's car is here, lights flashing, and for one irrational moment I hope that he is simply here to open the drawbridge. But that, of course, wouldn't explain the fact that three other squad cars are here as well. And so is the county van from the Medical Examiner's office. Jeff Skinner is standing behind the van's open rear doors, talking with the Chief and removing his surgical gloves. Whatever it is he's been doing here—he's finished.

I leave the Thunderbird behind the Chief's car and join them on the bridge. "What's going on, Chief?"

Chief Tommy Fitzpatrick looks like a cop. The lines etched in his face announce that he has lived every minute of his fifty-five years. He has a full head of strawberry blond hair and a broad, freckled face. Normally, his handshake is firm and his Irish eyes, like those in the song, are smiling. Not today, though.

He points to the side of the bridge. "Again," is all he says.

The feeling drains from my legs, but somehow they carry me to the bridge's wooden railing. On the marsh below, a fly rod is dropped haphazardly in the mud, its thin line broken and blowing in the salty breeze. A plastic fly box is tipped on its side, brightly colored flies glistening in the early morning sunlight. Striped bass are running now, and someone came here this morning intending to catch a few.

But that's not all. Three of Jeff's technicians are on the marsh too, combing everything in sight, using gloved hands to bag each glistening fly, and each section of the rod, individually. One of them even bags selected portions of pebbles and sand. And there is a body bag at the water's edge, all zipped up. It's not empty.

I turn back to the Chief and Jeff. "Why wasn't I called?"

The Chief looks surprised. "You were called," he says. "Or your office was called, anyhow."

Jeff speaks up. "Geraldine Schilling was here, Marty. She left about twenty minutes ago."

"Geraldine?" I stare at Jeff, open-mouthed. "Geraldine hasn't been to a crime scene in years."

"I know," he says. "But she was at this one."

Two of the technicians strain to lift the body bag from the marsh and drop it on a steel gurney. All three of them maneuver through the mud with some difficulty and lift the gurney over the lip of the wooden bridge. They roll it across the weathered planks toward the county van until I signal for them to stop. I brace myself, reach for the zipper at the top of the bag, and take a deep breath.

Jeff Skinner stops writing in his chart and hurries toward me, using his pen as a pointer, directing me away from the black vinyl bag. "Marty, don't do that," he says. "You need to trust me here, Marty. Don't open it."

The Chief backs him up. "Don't, Marty. Spare yourself, kid. Your office has it covered."

I have no interest in sparing myself. And I am not at all confident that my office has it covered. I unzip the bag and pull the stiff vinyl top back to expose the victim's head. My stomach turns over and my legs give out completely. I drop to my knees and vomit.

His skull is fractured. His throat is slit. His eyes are open.

Charlie Cahoon's precious grandson. Luke's friend. Jake Junior is dead.

Chapter 35

"For Christ's sake, you went to grade school with the victim's father. Your son played basketball with the victim himself. You don't belong on this case, Martha. It's too close."

Once again, Geraldine is on her feet, calling the shots. And Rob agrees with her. I can see it in his eyes.

"Marty," he pleads, "Geraldine is right. You loved Jake Junior. We all did. But you and Charlie are especially close. You can't handle this one. It wouldn't be right."

I feel an eerie sense of detachment, as if I am somewhere else, watching this scene play out from a distance. I will do what needs to be done, I tell myself, regardless of any decision Rob or Geraldine might make. And I won't argue with either one of them for long.

I don't recognize the person thinking those thoughts.

"Then who should handle it, Rob?"

My voice sounds unnaturally calm, even to me. Rob looks at me oddly before he answers. "Geraldine will first chair, and the Kydd will help her. It's time for him to cut his teeth on a real one anyhow."

"Geraldine is busy with the campaign, and I . . ."

"There won't be any campaign if this case is mishandled, Martha. The best thing I can do for the campaign is put Jacob Cahoon's murderer behind bars. And that's exactly what I intend to do."

Geraldine takes the cigarette out of her mouth and leans over my chair. The smoke curls from her left hand into my right eye as she bends down. "I will try this case. The Kydd will do the grunt work."

She leans closer to me. "And you, Martha," she says, "you will stay out of it."

I stand abruptly. Geraldine jumps back, but not quickly enough, and her cigarette falls on Rob's Oriental rug. I head for the door without apology. Geraldine is still talking, but I don't know—or care—what she is saying.

I stop in my office just long enough to retrieve my briefcase. The Kydd is coming through the office door as I head out.

"You leaving, Marty?"

"I have to, Kydd."

"That's okay. I can handle the docket."

"I know you can."

I weave through the crowd in the large lobby of the District Courthouse, out the front doors and into the glare of the morning sun. A dozen different attorneys approach me in the parking lot as I hurry toward the Thunderbird. A few want to offer condolences. Most want to work something out for whatever two-bit hoods they represent at the moment. I wave them all away.

I turn right out of the Barnstable County Complex. Five minutes later, I park between two vans in the Medical Examiner's lot. I open my glove compartment and retrieve an old point-and-shoot camera I keep there. The camera has a twenty-four-exposure roll of film in it, but twenty shots are used. Luke takes pictures of deer, coyote, and an occasional owl, whenever we happen upon them on Chatham's roads. That's okay. Four shots should do it.

I hold up my county I.D. card and stride past the guard at the front desk. He makes no attempt to stop me. I walk quickly down a long, sterile corridor, and let myself into the last room on the right, the room where I witnessed Skippy Eldridge's autopsy.

Two of the technicians are busy making preparations, one sterilizing the surgical instruments, the other filling out state-mandated paperwork. Jeff is not here yet. But the corpse is. In the corner of the room farthest from the door, the draped remains of Jake Junior rest on a padded gurney with stainless steel legs. My eyes fill and my vision blurs with the realization that the motionless heap on that table is all that is left of Jake Junior.

I cross the room quickly and retrieve a small, folded stepladder from its spot next to some hard-to-reach supply cabinets. The technician doing the paperwork is standing nearby, leaning on a stainless steel countertop. She is the young, innocent-looking woman who worked on Skippy Eldridge's autopsy. She smiles at me. "Nice to see you again, Attorney Nickerson. We were expecting Attorney Schilling on this one."

Her male counterpart is not nearly so gracious. He admonishes me from the other side of the room, tells me I should not be in the autopsy suite in street clothes. I should change into a sterile scrub suit at once, he says. I ignore him.

I put the stepladder next to the gurney, at Jake Junior's right side. I stand on its first rung and take two deep breaths to brace myself. I bend down and—quickly, so I can't change my mind—I remove the drape.

I am nauseated and unsteady as I step up to the second rung of the ladder, only vaguely aware that both technicians are gaping at me, motionless. I look through the camera's viewfinder and click once. I move the ladder to Jake Junior's feet and do it again. I repeat the process by his left side, and again by his head. Four shots in all, and the film automatically rewinds.

I am out the door. The young male technician is scolding me again when it closes. Something about the rules regarding appropriate garb in sterile areas. They exist for a reason, I think he said.

Harry's office is just another five-minute drive. He leads me to a small conference room and locks the door. The room is dimly lit. The shades are down, and the air is mercifully cool. Harry offers coffee, but I shake my head. "I can't. My stomach."

He pours a glass of water for me, sits in the chair next to mine, and takes my hands in his. "Marty, I'm so sorry."

Part of me wants to fall into his arms and stay there. But I can't. Instead I shake my head, take my hands back, retrieve the small cartridge of used film from my jacket pocket, and put it on the conference room table. I have to get through this quickly; I am going to be sick.

"Harry, do you have a film guy? Someone with a darkroom?"

"Yeah. A guy by the name of Kendall. I've used him for years."

"Do you trust him?"

"Yeah, I do, Marty. Why?"

"Have Mr. Kendall develop that. Please."

"Okay, that's easy. I'll take it to him today."

I am shaking. And I am losing the battle for my composure. Harry takes my hands back in his and sits quietly while I force some deep breaths. He doesn't ask until I look up at him.

"What's on it, Marty?"

"Twenty wildlife shots. Deer. Coyote. That sort of thing. Luke took them."

Harry nods patiently.

"And four shots that I took. Just now. In the morgue."

Harry leans close to me and brushes the damp hair from my fore-head. "Photos of Jake Junior," he says, trying to spare me as many words as he can.

"That's right. Jake Junior. With a Roman numeral three on his chest."

CHAPTER 36

Tuesday, June 15

Charlie Cahoon is dry-eyed today. He has no tears left. By the time I left him at midnight last night, he had cried an ocean. Dr. Paul O'Coyne, Charlie's physician and lifelong friend, brought medication to the house to help him sleep. Charlie wouldn't take it.

Before I left last night, I told Charlie that I would spend the day with him today. We will make the arrangements for Jake Junior together, I told him. We will schedule the visitation, the funeral, and the burial. We will call the out-of-town relatives and break the news. We'll let them know when the visitation and burial will be held. Charlie looked at me as if I were speaking in tongues.

I dropped Luke off at Chatham High School at the regular time this morning. There are no classes today, but a team of grief counselors will address the entire student body in the gymnasium. Afterward, the counselors will meet one-on-one with any student who so chooses.

I encouraged Luke to meet with one of the counselors, to try to talk about the dear friend he has lost. He said he would try. Never before have I seen such pain in his eyes. He is much older today than he was yesterday.

At eight, I called the office to say I wouldn't be coming in. I was surprised when Geraldine answered; she's not usually in the office that early. She sounded relieved when she heard what I had to say. I should take all the time I need, she told me, for my own sake as well as Charlie's. She and the Kydd are happy to cover for me.

Then I came here, to Charlie's house.

Charlie is wearing the same clothes he had on last night. And he is seated at the kitchen table, right where he was when I left. One look at him tells me he hasn't slept at all. I wonder if he has moved from that spot.

Charlie has an old-fashioned percolator on top of his gas stove. I fill its interior metal basket with coffee and put it on to perk. I wipe down the counters and wash the few dishes sitting in the sink—a ceramic cereal bowl, a spoon, and a Mason jar with a few drops of orange juice in it. Jake Junior had breakfast before he went bass fishing yesterday.

Once the coffee has perked, I pour a mug for each of us and join Charlie at the table. We sit in silence, Charlie staring into his mug as if he's never seen coffee before. A window by the table is open, and the birds singing outside seem out of place. Everything about the beautiful late spring day seems wrong.

Charlie is a member of Saint Christopher's Episcopal Church, a congregation that worships at a picturesque, white-steepled chapel on Main Street in Chatham. The priest, the Reverend Wallace Burrows, came by yesterday as soon as he heard what had happened to Jake Junior. But Charlie was unable to discuss arrangements; he was unable to speak at all.

"We should call Father Burrows first," I tell Charlie. "We should schedule the funeral, and the timing of the other arrangements will fall into place."

He just nods.

Charlie's telephone—one of the last rotary phones on earth, I'm sure—sits on a small pine desk in the corner of the kitchen. When I dial the office number for Saint Christopher's, Father Burrows answers the phone himself. He suggests Friday at ten for the funeral. I pass his suggestion along to Charlie, who agrees with a silent nod.

There is only one funeral parlor in Chatham and I dial that number next. Doane's Funeral Home, on Crowell Road, is available on Thursday night for the visitation. We should come by this afternoon to make the arrangements. The director will call the Medical Examiner's office and make sure the body can be released for burial.

Charlie has some family in the western part of Massachusetts, a couple of cousins and his wife's nephew. I ask where I might find their telephone numbers, and he points to the bottom drawer of the desk. As I flip through his small address book, it occurs to me that I may have done all of this too quickly for Charlie. He hasn't said a word all morning.

I turn back to the table and wait until he looks up at me. "Charlie, are these arrangements all right with you? Do you want to do anything differently?"

He looks into his coffee mug, as if the answer to my question might be floating in there. He clears his throat, but his voice is still gravelly from lack of use. "The arrangements are fine, Miss Marty. I appreciate all that you're doing. I've just been thinking—wondering—about what Harry Madigan said the day the judge threw him in jail—what he said about the numbers."

My eyes sting as the image of Jake Junior's mutilated torso appears—uninvited—before me. I turn away from Charlie abruptly and dial a cousin's number. I can't tell him. Not yet.

CHAPTER 37

Wednesday, June 16

Harry is sitting on the curb in front of my parking spot again. His tie is pulled down to the center of his shirt. His jacket is on the grass beside him, smashed underneath his briefcase. A plain manila envelope is on top of the closed briefcase. I know before I get out of the car that it holds the photographs of Jake Junior.

I lean against the hood and Harry hands me the envelope. The wildlife photos are bound together with a rubber band, a large coyote on top. The four photos of Jake Junior are loose. The first shot I took, from Jake Junior's right side, is out of focus. It's useless.

But the other three shots are clear. Each one shows a clean incision running from shoulder to shoulder and another from hip to hip. Three vertical incisions, uniform in depth, connect those two.

A small wave of nausea passes over me, and I sit down on the curb next to Harry. "Now what?" I ask him.

"Now we both know for sure," he says to the Thunderbird's front fender. "You and I both know that somebody is out there murdering young men and numbering them. We also know that somebody is tampering with evidence."

He turns to me and holds my eyes with his. "And whoever is doing the killing is also doing the tampering, Marty. Nothing else makes sense. Whoever this killer is, he or she has access to the Commonwealth's evidence."

My mind won't accept Harry's conclusion, but I have nothing to offer in rebuttal. Harry doesn't wait for an answer. "I have a guy—the same guy who developed your film, Kendall—he can set up some equipment for us. In the Commonwealth's evidence room; in the holding cells. A small camera and microphone in each."

I am having trouble following this. "Harry, what are you saying?"

"I'm saying we should set up surveillance, Marty. And we should do it right now. When the cops bag somebody for Jake Junior's murder, we need to see who doctors the evidence to guarantee a conviction. Too many people have access to the Commonwealth's evidence. You know that. Cops, lawyers, lab people, probably the janitor, for Christ's sake. We've got to nail this bastard."

Harry talks to the Thunderbird's fender again. "Kendall has the equipment. He'll install it. But you've got the keys. You've got to get us into the evidence room and the holding cells."

My head is splitting. "Harry, I can't do that. I can't plant surveillance equipment in my own office. Let me talk to Rob. I never got a chance to talk to him on Monday. I wanted to tell him . . ."

"For Christ's sake, Marty, we can't trust even them. Rob doesn't pour a cup of coffee without consulting Geraldine. And, even assuming the best, Geraldine won't face up to any fact that might damage her goddamned campaign. You think she'll acknowledge the possibility of a serial killer at this point? She'd have to admit that the Rodriguez conviction is bogus, and that the evidence being offered against Eddie Malone was manufactured by somebody—and not just anybody: an insider. She won't do that, Marty. You know that as well as I do."

Harry stands, so I do too. He grabs me by the shoulders and plants his face close to mine. "Marty, we don't have time to waste. If the cops bag somebody tonight, the evidence that will convict him will be in place by tomorrow morning. And do you know what that means, Marty? Do you?"

I know what that means, but I can't say it. Harry says it for me. "Number four."

CHAPTER 38

Thursday, June 17

From the custodians to the judges, those who staff the Barnstable County Complex turn out to mourn Jake Junior. Most of the year-round population of Chatham is here as well. Doane's Funeral Parlor is filled to capacity, and the line stretches out the door and halfway down Crowell Road. Charlie is overwhelmed by the outpouring of love and support.

Visiting hours are scheduled from seven to nine this evening, but it will take much longer than that to accommodate this number of mourners. By eight o'clock, Charlie is visibly exhausted, and the line is still out the door. At my request, the director sets up a half dozen folding chairs at one end of the room, not far from Jake Junior's plain white coffin. Charlie and I sit in two of the chairs and the visitors sit with us in small groups to convey their sympathies to Charlie. I hold his hand and keep his water glass filled.

Rob, Justin, and Jeff arrive together, but their visit with Charlie is short. Justin's eyes are swollen and bloodshot. When he hugs Charlie, they both break down completely. Afterward, Rob and Jeff try to steer Justin away from Jake Junior's coffin, but he won't let them.

Justin falls to his knees in front of the white box, lays his wet cheek against the smooth wood, and throws both arms across the coffin's closed lid. Luke crosses the room, kneels next to him, and puts his own long arms around Justin's shoulders. Rob and Jeff step back from them, looking helpless.

Luke and Justin have always leaned on each other through life's difficulties. They have never faced one of this magnitude before, but they will get through it together, the only way they know.

After Rob, Justin, and Jeff leave the funeral parlor, the line moves more quickly. Each group visits with Charlie just briefly, then moves to the coffin, where most of them make the sign of the cross and drop to the velvet-covered kneeler to pray for Jake Junior.

The coffin is closed, of course, because of the damage to Jake Junior's skull and the slit in his throat. But next to the closed white box is a wooden easel, with an enlarged color photograph of Jake Junior and Charlie. Luke put it there.

Luke took the photo after this season's final basketball game. Chatham won the game, and Jake Junior is beaming. He is a foot taller than his grandfather, and his smile shows the familiar little gap between his two front teeth. He has the basketball tucked under his left arm, and his right arm encircles his grandfather's shoulders. Charlie is beaming too.

Luke is standing behind the easel, bidding good night to the mourners as they leave. All on his own, he has assumed the role of a host here, thanking those who have turned out to honor the memory of his fallen friend.

It's almost midnight when the funeral director escorts us all to the front door. Luke climbs into the backseat of the Thunderbird, leaving the front passenger door open for Charlie. Charlie, still virtually sleepless since the murder, offered no protest when I suggested that I do the driving tonight for both of us.

The only traffic light on Main Street is at the intersection of Crowell Road. It's red when we get there. I stop and look over at Charlie, who hasn't said a word since bidding farewell to the last mourner. There are tears in his eyes.

Charlie looks back at me and shakes his head. "They loved him," he says, his voice weak and wavering. "All those people. In all my days, I've never seen anything like it. They really loved Jake Junior."

I reach over and put my hand on his. "They still do," I tell him. "And they love you, too."

Charlie's tears flow freely as I turn left on Main Street. He doesn't say anything else until I stop in front of his white clapboard house on Bridge Street. He pauses before getting out of the car, and turns toward me with a troubled look on his face.

"Miss Marty, you've been so good to me. I hate to ask you for anything else. I hate to do it. But I don't know who else to ask."

I hold up my hand to stop his apology. "Name it, Charlie. You know that. Just name it."

"Well, tomorrow, at the service . . ."

"What, Charlie?"

"Well, usually, someone gets up and says something about the person. You know, about his life."

"You mean the eulogy?"

"That's it, the eulogy. Well, I don't know who to ask, Miss Marty. It's been just Jake Junior and me for so long. And the good Lord knows I can't speak in public. I wouldn't remember my own name if I stood up to speak. It wouldn't be right for Jake Junior."

I'm about to tell Charlie to stop worrying, that I will be happy to say a few words about Jake Junior. But Luke speaks up first, leaning forward in the back seat.

"Mr. Cahoon, if it would be all right with you . . . well, I'd be honored to give the eulogy for Jake Junior."

Charlie turns and faces him. Tears stream down Charlie's face, but he actually smiles. "Oh, Luke," he says, "I would be so grateful."

CHAPTER 39

Friday, June 18

Main Street is closed to general traffic from Veterans' Circle eastward. Only those cars and trucks headed to Jake Junior's funeral are permitted through. Troopers posted at the rotary divert all other traffic north on Old Harbor Road, or south toward the Oyster Pond. Even so, Main Street is choked with cars and pedestrians.

The interior of Saint Christopher's chapel is rustic, almost Spartan. There is a plain wooden altar at the front of the room, and a simple pulpit to the left of it. The wooden pews are honey-colored; their kneelers are not padded. Prayer books and hymnals rest in matching wooden racks on the back of each pew.

The easel bearing the photograph of Charlie and Jake Junior stands next to the pulpit. Luke and I picked it up from the funeral parlor early this morning, when we drove Charlie there for his last few moments alone with Jake Junior's remains. The photo provides the only splash of color in the church.

Charlie's final moments with Jake Junior's body siphoned the last of his reserves. When Luke and I pulled up to his house on Bridge Street, he emerged with a brown shopping bag, and he clutched it on his lap during the short ride to the funeral home. He carried it inside and set it down carefully on the kneeler next to Jake Junior's coffin. When the director lifted the coffin's white lid, Charlie fell to his knees beside the bag and sobbed. Luke and I stood behind him, helpless.

We couldn't stand for long, though. The morticians had done all they could with Jake Junior's corpse. They placed his head on the small satin pillow at an angle that minimized our view of his skull damage. They buttoned his shirt to the top and pulled it upward on his neck, covering most of the narrow slit in his throat. Still, the sight of Jake Junior, lifeless, brought Luke and me to our knees.

We sank to the carpeted floor, behind Charlie and his paper bag, until Charlie grew silent. The funeral director handed him one end of a soft white sheet, then, offering him the opportunity to cover his grandson for the last time, before the coffin's lid would close for good. Charlie stood and accepted the sheet, but he didn't cover Jake Junior, not then, anyway. Instead, he stroked Jake Junior's forehead, and ran his hand down the front of Jake Junior's suit jacket. When he reached inside the coffin, toward Jake Junior's rigid right hand, I panicked.

For just a split second, I thought Charlie had decided to examine Jake Junior's chest, to answer for himself the question I wouldn't answer for him three days ago. But I was wrong. Charlie made no move toward Jake Junior's torso. Instead, he held Jake Junior's right hand in his own for several moments, then placed it down just long enough to reach into his brown shopping bag.

His basketball. Charlie took it from the bag and tucked it next to Jake Junior, under his right forearm. He nodded up at the funeral director, then, and together they covered Jake Junior and his basketball for the last time. Luke and I each took one of Charlie's arms afterward, and the three of us walked in silence back to the Thunderbird.

The chapel is filled beyond capacity. The usher leads Luke, Charlie, and me to the front pew, which has been roped off and saved for us. Harry ducks through the side door, waves to us, and disappears into the crowd standing in the back. Loudspeakers are set up outside the church, so that those who can get no closer than the sidewalk will at least be able to hear Jake Junior's service.

The back doors open and the priest begins the solemn words of the service. Six members of the varsity basketball team, all juniors and seniors, carry Jake Junior's white coffin down the center aisle. Justin is one of them. He is in front, on our side of the aisle. Charlie breaks down again beside me. I take his hand and hold it in both of mine.

Once the coffin is in place on an elevated platform in the center aisle, the pallbearers file into the pew across from ours. The remainder of the basketball team is standing along the far wall. I look across the center aisle, past the coffin, and offer a small smile to Justin, who is in the end seat. Justin nods back at me, his sore eyes running like faucets. Rob is seated behind him, keeping a reassuring hand on his son's shoulder.

Father Burrows leads us in the ancient and comforting words of the service. He tells us to sit, and he reads three passages from scripture. He delivers a homily on the mysteries surrounding our lives and our deaths. He acknowledges our inability to comprehend an event like Jake Junior's tragic end. He recognizes our feelings of anger, hopelessness, and despair. God is here, he tells us. God will help us through our grief.

Charlie shakes his head. "I don't know, Miss Marty," he whispers.

"I think God has just plain turned his back on the people of Chatham."

I squeeze his hand.

Luke stands and walks to the pulpit. He is wearing a suit we bought a few months ago for the basketball awards banquet, and it's too small for him already. The sleeves are an inch and a half too short. He doesn't seem to care.

Luke faces the crowded church. He has a few pages of notes, but he doesn't look at them. He nods to Charlie and me, then looks beyond us to what must be an ocean of sorrowful faces.

"This past Monday," he begins, his voice shaking a little, "the sun rose over Stage Harbor just like it always does. It looked like another beautiful morning on Cape Cod. But it wasn't. It was a black morning, a morning we will never forget, a morning that brought with it the abrupt end of a great young life."

Luke stares down at his hands and swallows hard before he looks up again. "For those of us who loved Jake Junior, the world stopped turning that morning."

Luke's voice is strong and steady now. He looks toward the coffin in the center aisle. "And the world will never be the same again."

Charlie is crying hard, but there is a small smile on his face as he nods up at Luke. He wants these words to be said, painful though they are to hear.

"Everybody knows that Jake Junior was a great basketball player. But those of us who were lucky enough to be Jake Junior's friends, lucky enough to be part of his everyday life, we know he was a lot more than that. We know he was a great human being.

"Jake Junior was good to everybody. Not just to his friends and teammates, but to everybody. When a new guy came to our school last term, Jake Junior was the first to sit with him in the cafeteria. And because Jake Junior joined him, the rest of us joined him too. Just like that, the new guy had a whole bunch of friends."

Luke looks directly at Charlie. "He made the rest of us better people."

Charlie continues to cry silently, nodding at Luke.

"Jake Junior had an iron will. If he missed a shot during a basketball game, which he didn't do often . . ."

Soft laughter ripples through the church, a small and welcome relief.

". . . you'd find him in the gym the next day, taking that shot over and over again. Next game . . ."

Luke smiles and raises both hands as if taking a shot.

". . . nothing but net."

This ripple of laughter is louder. More relief.

"And coupled with that iron will was a great big generous heart. If you needed a favor—no matter what it was—Jake Junior was right there. If you needed advice—no matter what about—Jake Junior was right there. He'd fill you in on teachers, coaches, and—sometimes—girls."

Everybody laughs. Even Charlie chuckles through his tears.

"And, oh boy, did Jake Junior love basketball. If he wasn't playing basketball, he was trying to put a pick-up game together. And if the Celtics were on television, Jake Junior wouldn't let anyone else have the remote."

Another ripple of laughter. More precious relief.

Luke reaches over the side of the pulpit and takes the photograph from its perch on the wooden easel. "But more than anything, Jake Junior loved his grandfather."

Charlie catches his breath, and I squeeze his hand again. I have always been proud of Luke, but never more so than at this moment.

"Jake Junior told me once, about a year ago, that he couldn't remember anything about his mom or dad. He'd seen pictures and heard stories, but he didn't have any memories of his own. When I said I was sorry, that it must be rough to not have folks, Jake Junior was surprised."

Luke looks directly at Charlie. "I still remember what he said to me that day. He said, 'Gosh, Luke, don't feel sorry for me. I live with the greatest guy on earth.'"

Charlie's shoulders are shaking, but he is smiling. His eyes are riveted to Luke.

"And I remember what he was doing while we had that conversation. He was fixing up an old bicycle, one he had outgrown years before. He said he had heard about a kid in the sixth grade who rode his bike to school every day until somebody stole it. Jake Junior was fixing up his old bike to give to him.

"When I asked who the sixth-grader was, Jake Junior said he didn't know his name. Then I asked a really dumb question. I said, 'Jake Junior, if you don't even know the kid's name, why are you giving him a bike?' Jake Junior shrugged, and you know what he said?"

The crowd is still; the church is silent.

"He said, 'Because it feels like the right thing to do.'"

Luke takes a minute to put the photo of Jake Junior and Charlie back on the easel. He looks out at the crowd and takes a deep breath.

"Early last fall, Jake Junior went to a Saturday meeting for high school seniors interested in the army's college credit program. Obviously, that was before he got his scholarship from Duke."

The congregation laughs again.

"He came back from that Saturday meeting with a dozen identical tee shirts. One for himself, and one for every other member of the varsity basketball team. They are plain white tee shirts, with 'United States Army' written in small letters across the front. But that wasn't what Jake Junior liked about them. What grabbed him was what was written in larger letters on the back. The army's slogan: 'Be all that you can be.'

"He was. More than anyone I have ever known, Jake Junior was all that he could be. He was wearing that shirt—and those words—the morning he died.

"That is Jake Junior's legacy. He taught me—and everybody else who knew him—to be all that we can be. To do all that we can do, even when the rest of the world doesn't expect it from us. To do all that we can do, just because that's the right way to live. And if we keep Jake Junior's legacy alive, then his spirit will live on in each one of us."

Luke leaves the pulpit and walks back to our pew. Charlie stands and embraces him. They are frozen. For the first time today, I break down.

Father Burrows says a final blessing over the coffin. The organist begins the recessional hymn. The pallbearers take their places and lift the coffin up over their shoulders. We follow them down the aisle and outside, where the Chatham fog has taken over Main Street.

Luke and I stand with Charlie on the steps of the church while the pallbearers load the coffin into the polished gray hearse and close its rear double doors. Harry comes out of the chapel and stands next to me.

"I'll do it," I tell him. "Call Mr. Kendall. We'll set up the surveillance equipment this weekend."

"Are you sure?"

"I'm sure."

"Why, Marty? Why did you change your mind?"

I look up at him. "Because it feels like the right thing to do, Harry. And I have to do all that I can do."

CHAPTER 40

Sunday, June 20

Father's Day has always been a challenge. For years, Luke pretended not to notice the holiday. He'd say since his father ignored him all year, he should ignore his father on Father's Day. But I always knew it weighed on him.

Last year was especially awkward. Luke's first visit with Ralph was over the Memorial Day weekend, and three weeks later we were shopping for a Father's Day gift. "I don't even know the man," Luke kept saying as we rummaged through the men's department of Puritan Clothing Store. Each time he said it, the saleswoman arched her eyebrows and cast a disapproving frown at me over her rhinestone-studded half-glasses.

This year is better. Luke announced last Sunday night, after watching the Red Sox trounce the New York Yankees at Fenway Park, that he wanted to get a pair of tickets to another Sox game and give them to Ralph for Father's Day. That's giving a gift you'd like to receive, I told him. Actually, it's giving a gift you will receive, which must be worse.

Nonetheless, I thought it was a good idea. More important, it was Luke's idea, and not mine. We ordered the tickets first thing Monday morning, before we left the house for work and school, before we were aware of what had happened beneath the Mitchell River Bridge, before our world turned upside down.

We tried to get tickets for today, Father's Day, but they were sold out. We settled on a pair of tickets for a home game against the Seattle Mariners next Saturday night. And it's just as well. The events of the past week have left Luke drained. I'm used to death, though not the death of a young friend, but for someone Luke's age, such a death is devastating. He spent most of yesterday on the beach behind our cottage with Danny Boy, halfheartedly skipping stones through the waves. He left our property only once—to walk the beaches of the Monomoy Wildlife Refuge with Justin. Neither of them wanted to be far from the familiar sounds of the ocean, Luke said.

Luke normally sleeps in on Sundays, but he agreed to set his alarm clock and get up in time to go to a Father's Day breakfast with Ralph at nine today. Ralph is flying into the Chatham Municipal Airport again on a small chartered plane. He'll spend a few hours with Luke, then fly back into Logan where, once again, he'll catch a commercial flight to Seattle. He doesn't have a choice; he's been recalled to the stand in the Dr. Wu trial.

Technically, every trial witness is subject to being recalled later in the trial if subsequent evidence raises a new issue that the witness should address. As a practical matter, though, witness recalls almost never happen. Trial judges expect the attorneys on both sides of a case to get every piece of information they might need from a witness the first time he testifies. Only when the subsequent evidence is truly a surprise—one that couldn't have been anticipated by the attorney requesting the recall—is the recall granted. This past Friday, a recall of Ralph was granted to the attorneys prosecuting Dr. Wu.

According to the press, the final witness for the defense was Willie Chung himself. Mr. Chung has no criminal record and, by all accounts, he did a credible job on the witness stand. Over and over again he denied playing any role whatsoever in any of the five murders. Even under grueling cross-examination, he professed ignorance of the methods of homicide used by Dr. Wu. His testimony provided the necessary factual backup for Ralph's expert psychiatric opinion that Chung couldn't be held criminally responsible for the conduct of Dr. Wu.

The prosecutor cross-examined Willie Chung for the better part of three days. He had all but wrapped it up when he asked the question that elicited the surprise testimony. "Dr. Ellis is an expensive expert witness," he said to Mr. Chung. "Where did you get the money to pay for him?"

The fees charged by expert witnesses are fair game in all trials, civil and criminal. A jury is entitled to conclude, if it so chooses, that the expert's opinion has more to do with the sum of money he's being paid than with his professional evaluation of the facts. Any competent cross-examination of an expert witness calls for disclosure of the expert's hourly rates. The cross-examination of Ralph was no exception.

Ralph recited his rates to the court matter-of-factly during his cross-examination, and his testimony was broadcast on the evening news. He charges four hundred dollars an hour for reviewing medical records and other documents. The same rate applies to travel time. His rate rises to five hundred for each hour of deposition testimony and each hour spent clinically evaluating a patient. The rate tops out at six hundred dollars for each hour of courtroom testimony.

Further cross-examination elicited the fact that Willie Chung had paid Ralph a one-hundred-thousand-dollar retainer, and had replenished it promptly on two separate occasions when it fell below the fifty-thousand mark. The checks were drawn on Chung's personal account, Ralph testified.

It was only natural, then, that the prosecutor would wonder how a man who made his living doling out herbal remedies came up with such a staggering sum of money. The defense attorneys should have anticipated as much. Apparently, though, they did not.

Willie Chung was thrown by the question. In the portion of his testimony that aired on the news he stammered and coughed, then testified that the money had come from a friend. "A very generous friend," he said. After further questioning, Chung explained that the friend had wired the funds into Chung's personal account to pay the initial retainer, and again each time he needed to replenish it. When the prosecutor asked Chung to identify his generous friend, the defense attorneys went through the roof.

After a lengthy sidebar, the presiding judge ordered Willie Chung to answer the question. During the pause that followed, the lead prosecutor employed one of the oldest trial tactics known to litigators. He pulled a sheaf of documents from his briefcase and leafed through it—looking smug—while waiting patiently for Chung's answer. The prosecutor's performance was intended to suggest to Chung that the government already knew the identity of the generous friend, and had the documentation to prove it. It worked.

After minutes of deafening silence, Willie Chung leaned forward in the witness stand and said into the microphone, "Lester Pan." Those two words launched pandemonium in the courtroom, a scene the eleven o'clock news aired three times. It seems that Lester Pan is well known in the Pacific Northwest as the dictator of a small but powerful faction of the Chinese mob. He specializes in importing illegal immigrants from China, almost all of them underage females.

But that's not all. Lester Pan is also the sole suspect in the murder of an immigration officer who got too close for Pan's comfort. He remains a suspect—rather than a defendant—because the intimidated witnesses won't talk and, without them, prosecutors can't convict. All in all, Lester Pan does not seem to be a man who would help Willie Chung—or anyone else, for that matter—out of the goodness of his heart.

The revelation of Willie Chung's mob connection puts Ralph in a terrible spot. If he testifies that he knew Lester Pan to be the source of his retainer payments, he will appear to have been less than forthcoming when he testified that the money came straight from Chung's personal account. His overall credibility will be damaged. He will be seen as an advocate, rather than as an unbiased psychiatrist. The jury might discredit his testimony altogether.

On the other hand, if Ralph testifies that he knew nothing of Lester Pan, then it will seem that Ralph's patient was able to outwit him, hiding potentially important information from him. If Chung successfully hid his mob ties from Ralph, he may have hidden other important facts as well. He might even have hidden facts that would prove he has firsthand knowledge of the murders. Ralph's diagnosis, then, will be rendered meaningless.

Ralph taps on the kitchen door and lets himself in promptly at nine. His expression—usually self-satisfied—is anxious and tense. He knows he is in for brutal questioning this week. I decide not to touch it.

Luke is ready on time again and, within minutes, they are out the kitchen door. I sit on the back deck with Danny Boy just long enough to finish my coffee. I am headed out myself this morning. I'm meeting Harry at ten o'clock outside the Barnstable District Courthouse. He won't be alone.

Chapter 41

Mr. Kendall is an odd-looking man and that appears to be a matter of choice. He is taller than Harry by about three inches, and painfully thin. He is dressed all in black, from the tam on his head to the shiny toes of his wing tips, in spite of the summer sun. He carries two large equipment bags, both solid black with no markings of any kind. He puts one of them down as I walk toward the side entrance to the courthouse, and extends a chalk white hand equipped with extraordinarily long, tapered fingers.

"Attorney Nickerson," he says, "I'm pleased to meet you. I've seen you on the news so many times. I'm Bobo Kendall."

Bobo shakes my hand so hard my shoulder hurts.

"Please," I say, "call me Marty."

I wonder, though, if I will be able to call a grown man Bobo.

Harry takes my hand after Bobo lets go. "How're you doing?" he asks.

"I'm okay."

"How's Luke?"

"Better. He had a quiet day yesterday, and he needed it. He's at breakfast with Ralph right now."

Harry holds on to my hand, but leans toward Bobo and arches his eyebrows. "Ralph is the psychiatrist ex-husband," he says. "Talk about a guy who needs his head examined."

My cheeks grow hot instantly. I brush past both of them and fumble with my keys at the side door. Once inside, Harry and Bobo are astute enough to keep a distance while I enter the four-digit code that prevents the alarm from sounding. I hope my color is returning to normal when I turn to face them. "Where do we start?" I ask Bobo.

"Your office," he says. "I'll look around in there first, then size up the holding cells and the evidence room."

I am surprised that my office is part of this plan, but I realize at once that I shouldn't be. If we record what goes on in the holding cells and the evidence room, we'll need someplace to watch that footage. I don't expect Geraldine will volunteer her office. Mine is the only option.

The side entrance to the District Courthouse opens to the level below the main floor. Bobo leaves his equipment bags inside the door. I lead the way up one flight of stairs, across the large lobby with its familiar stale smell, and take out my keys again to open the outer door to our offices. I am oddly aware of the black block lettering on the door's frosted glass. BARNSTABLE COUNTY DISTRICT ATTORNEY'S OFFICE, it says. It is as if I am seeing it for the first time. I wonder if Ethel Rosenberg had a similar moment.

Bobo takes less than ten minutes to learn all he needs to know about my small office. I lead him and Harry back down the stairs, two flights this time, to the bowels of the building. The District Court's holding cells are at one end of a poorly lit, institutional green corridor; the Commonwealth's evidence room is at the other. We survey the barren holding cells first, then head toward the evidence room. I find the key on my key ring, jiggle it up and down in the stubborn lock the way I've done so many times before, and walk in front of Bobo and Harry into the sickly smell of the Commonwealth's evidence.

The place is a mess. It's never been cleaned out during the time I've worked here, and a complete inventory hasn't been taken since Rob was first elected a dozen years ago. Banker's boxes are stacked to the ceiling against all four walls; most, but not all, are labeled with case names and docket numbers. The dust and cobwebs on them tell all of us they haven't been touched in years.

The evidence from more recent cases is stored on freestanding metal shelving units set up in the middle of the large room. Plastic crates stuffed with evidence bags are arranged in rough chronological order from left to right. Three crates on the middle shelf hold the evidence from the Rodriguez trial. To the right of them is a single crate marked MALONE. It holds only five evidence bags, one for Eddie's trousers, one for each of his socks, and one for each of his sneakers. The evidence taken from Skippy Eldridge's corpse hasn't made its way here from the morgue yet.

There is no crate set up for the most recent murder. No arrest has been made, and the evidence taken from Jake Junior's body is still in the lab. I wonder what we will do when these metal shelving units are filled. We might be forced to clean house.

Bobo leaves the room without a word. He returns minutes later with the two equipment bags. He opens both and takes stock of their contents before he begins. One holds a dozen miniature cameras, twice as many microphones, and yards of insulated wire. The other holds every type of tool I have ever seen and a few that I haven't. If

Bobo ever tires of surveillance work, he can always go rob the nearest savings and loan.

Harry makes himself comfortable on the floor, leaning against a stack of banker's boxes. I pull one of the boxes from the stack next to his and use it for a chair in the midst of the clutter, a few yards from Bobo's bags. Bobo selects a small flat implement from one of them, a tool similar to one Sergeant Carmine used to open the door to the Thunderbird when I locked the keys inside, something she referred to as a slim jim.

Bobo uses the slim jim to remove a strip of vertical paneling from between two stacks of banker's boxes. With a sharp blade, he cuts out a chunk of insulation from the space behind the panel. He selects a tiny camera, a gunmetal gray Sony, and bolts it to the wooden laths of the wall. He runs wires from the camera's base up the laths and behind the room's suspended ceiling.

Bobo does some measuring and, using a battery-operated drill, he bores a round hole in the strip of paneling he removed. When the hole is precisely the size of the camera's lens, Bobo spreads a small amount of adhesive on the back side of the panel and returns it to the wall, aligning the small drilled hole with the lens. The hole is little more than an inch in diameter. It would never be noticed by anyone who isn't searching for it.

Next, Bobo reaches up and easily removes a fiberglass square from the suspended ceiling. He bores a hole roughly the same size as the one in the wall panel, and inserts a tiny microphone in the opening. He joins the microphone's wiring to the camera's, and returns the fiberglass square to its rightful spot overhead. Just like that, we are done in the evidence room.

Bobo repeats essentially the same process in each of the half dozen holding cells, with only one real difference. Both the camera and the microphone are planted in the ceiling of each small cell, since the concrete walls offer no hospitality to Bobo's equipment. When he finishes, the three of us return to my office. Bobo sizes up my old wooden file cabinet and points to the dull brass hardware at the top. "Does this thing lock?"

I tell him it does, fish through my top desk drawer, and hand him the key. He opens the top drawer of the file cabinet, lifts out the files, and hands them to me. "Can you put these somewhere else?" he asks.

Bobo is obviously unfamiliar with the budget constraints of the District Attorney's office. I can't remember the last time I had extra space for files in my office. But I know who does. "I think I can," I tell Bobo.

I leave Harry and Bobo and head down the hall to the Kydd's office, a space even smaller than mine. He spent Memorial Day weekend cleaning out the solitary file cabinet in his office while we waited for the Rodriguez verdict. He won't mind if I rent space for a while. Sure enough, the bottom drawer of his cabinet is empty. I deposit my files there, and make a mental note to give the Kydd some explanation in the morning.

By the time I get back to my office, Bobo is just about finished setting up a midsized monitor in the top drawer of the old file cabinet, an odd-looking home for such a high-tech device. Just as quickly, he assembles a small speaker next to it. He spends the next two hours tapping into the building's existing wiring, adding to it, and connecting my file cabinet to the rooms we will monitor, two floors below.

Bobo sends Harry back to the evidence room to stand in place in front of the metal shelving unit. I watch with Bobo as Harry comes into view in front of the Rodriguez evidence, the Malone evidence, and a bit of empty space on the right. Harry stares directly into the camera, deadpan. "Smile," he says flatly. "You're on *America's Most Wanted*."

Harry's image is somewhat distorted. Bobo leaves my office and appears minutes later on the monitor. I stand by the cabinet and watch both Harry and Bobo disappear from view before a muffled static comes through the speaker in the drawer. Moments later, they are back on screen, their images crystal clear now. Bobo tells Harry to stay put and, minutes later, is back in my office. He appears satisfied with our view of the evidence room.

Bobo and Harry repeat the test in all six holding cells, Bobo making three separate trips down the stairs to adjust cameras and microphones. Once he is satisfied with those rooms, Bobo teaches Harry and me how to handle the equipment in my office. It's simple, even for me, and Luke describes me as technologically challenged.

Each of the rooms being monitored has its own channel. By setting the monitor to channel one, we can see and hear all activity in the evidence room. By changing to channels two through seven, we can see and hear the activity in each of the six holding cells.

Each camera stores twenty-four hours' worth of footage, then begins taping over on the same film. If we get to the camera two hours after the suspect is locked in a holding cell, we simply rewind the film by 120 minutes, and we can view what happened in his cell before we arrived. A digital display in the lower right corner tells us what time the events we're watching actually took place, right down to the second.

It's good there are two of us, Bobo says. One of us can review time past, if necessary, while the other—in person—keeps an eye on the present. Using a panel of dials on the base of the monitor, we can rewind, fast forward, and even zoom in.

Bobo locks the cabinet's top drawer and drops the key into my open hand. "My work is done here," he says.

The key in my palm looks different somehow. In fact, my whole office seems changed. The explanation dawns on me as the three of us walk together across the darkened courthouse lobby. I am not on my old team anymore. I have joined the other side.

CHAPTER 42

Tuesday, June 22

Judge Gould called a thirty-minute recess after we finished the regular docket at one-thirty. Eddie Malone's competency hearing will begin at two. The Kydd and I handled this morning's docket together, and I invited him to stay with me at the counsel table for the next hearing. The Kydd hasn't seen a competency hearing yet, and in Judge Gould's courtroom, he will see one handled properly.

Eddie Malone was transported to the Barnstable County House of Correction from Bridgewater State Hospital this morning, in plenty of time to be present for the proceedings. If Judge Gould finds that Eddie is competent to stand trial, his arraignment will reconvene immediately after the hearing. If Judge Gould finds otherwise, Eddie will probably be shipped back to the hospital for further evaluation. In light of the report issued by the Bridgewater staff, the arraignment will almost certainly go forward.

Judge Gould's referring order directed the physicians at Bridgewater to evaluate Eddie Malone's competency to stand trial as well as his potential for criminal responsibility at the time he allegedly murdered Skippy Eldridge. The doctors' report was issued yesterday in anticipation of today's hearing. In it the attending psychiatrist describes Eddie's condition at three different points in his commitment.

Seven days after Eddie's admission to Bridgewater, the psychiatrist describes him as "functioning on a low to average level of intelligence." The doctor classifies his judgment and insight as "very poor." Eddie's memory, the doctor says, is "substantially impaired."

A week later, the doctor notes that Eddie shows "some insight" into his problems. Further, "with coaching" Eddie appears to understand the precise nature of the charges leveled against him, as well as the evidence supporting those charges. Finally, the report concludes with a diagnosis entered yesterday. "Mental Deficiency. IQ 73. Mild to Moderate."

The attending psychiatrist goes on to express the opinion that, despite Eddie's mental deficiency, he is competent to stand trial. Furthermore, the doctor opines, Eddie was "mentally and criminally responsible" on May 31. His "mental deficiency," according to the doctor, did not render him "mentally incompetent."

Harry took over the defense table as soon as Judge Gould left the bench. He is armed with the affidavits from Shirley Donaldson, Ricky Sparrow, and the nicest lady on Cape Cod, Laurie Griffin. Just this morning, he filed an emergency motion to dismiss the charges against Eddie, arguing that the evidence we are offering against him had to have been staged. Judge Gould will hear the motion before Eddie's competency hearing begins.

Because of the emergency timing of Harry's motion and the size of this morning's docket, I have prepared only an oral opposition to Harry's motion to dismiss. There was no time to put it in writing. Even so, Harry doesn't expect to win. He does, though, expect the press to run with it.

And the press appears prepared to do so. They are here in record numbers—reporters, TV camera operators, still photographers—from all over New England. They jockey for position and create a ruckus when the guards lead Eddie Malone into the courtroom. They shout questions at both Eddie and Harry. Eddie doesn't respond at all. Harry tells them he'll be glad to speak with all of them after the hearing.

The bailiff calls the room to order and Judge Gould resumes his position on the bench. Harry and I remain standing when everyone else sits down. Each of us takes a few steps toward the bench, but we pause to give Judge Gould time to open his file and adjust his glasses. He looks up and nods first at me, then at Harry, indicating he is ready to hear from Harry first, since he is the moving party.

But it's not Harry's voice that fills the courtroom.

"Geraldine Schilling for the Commonwealth, Your Honor."

She strides down the courtroom's center aisle and points her index finger from me to the chair, telling me to sit down. I walk back to the counsel table, my face instantly red, and slip clumsily into the chair beside the Kydd. He is as surprised as I am; he's never seen Geraldine open her mouth in a courtroom. She hasn't done any active trial work for about four years. But she doesn't seem to have lost her flair for the dramatic.

"The physicians at Bridgewater State Hospital have completed their evaluation of Edmund Malone, Your Honor. Your Honor has a copy of the report. Edmund Malone is competent to stand trial. Further, he understood and appreciated the wrongful nature of his conduct on the morning in question."

Geraldine is holding her own copy of the Bridgewater report. But she doesn't have the rest of the file. I do. I wonder if she realizes that Harry has filed a motion to dismiss.

"The Commonwealth asks that this case be scheduled for trial posthaste and that defendant Edmund Malone be held until that time, without bail, in the Barnstable County House of Correction."

Judge Gould is visibly annoyed. He looks from me to Geraldine three different times and it's clear, to me at least, that he is not happy about Geraldine's theatrical entrance. He peers down at her over the dark rims of his glasses.

"That's all well and good, Ms. Schilling, but there is a motion to dismiss pending before this court."

Geraldine is caught off guard. "A motion to dismiss? On what grounds?"

There is a swell of noise in the gallery, including a fair amount of laughter. Judge Gould pounds his gavel and calls for order. He is downright angry now. "Ms. Schilling, you just marched into this courtroom and announced that you represent the Commonwealth in this matter. Yet you are unaware of the defendant's motion to dismiss?"

Geraldine is wearing an expression I have never before seen on her face. She is mortified. She walks backward toward the counsel table, keeping her eyes on the judge, and signals for me to stand. I stay put.

Geraldine is stammering, something I've never before heard from her. "Oh, Your Honor . . . my colleague, Ms. Nickerson . . . She is handling that aspect of the case."

Geraldine signals frantically for me to abandon my chair. I don't move. Finally, she unglues her eyes from Judge Gould and glares at me, panic-stricken. I sit still just long enough to consider the ramifications of my decision.

I heave the Malone file at Geraldine and she grabs it in self-defense. I lift my briefcase from the floor to the table and stand to address the court. "Attorney Schilling is mistaken, Your Honor. I am not handling any aspect of the case against Mr. Malone. Ms. Schilling represents the Commonwealth."

Geraldine freezes. The Kydd's lower jaw goes slack. The reporters buzz. I take my briefcase from the counsel table and push my way past them. I'm gone.

CHAPTER 43

Wednesday, June 23

Geraldine is not a morning person. Most days, she gets to the office a full hour after I do. Most days, she closes the door to her office—hard—as soon as she gets in. Most days, she ignores the rest of us until about noontime.

Not today, though.

Geraldine's reserved parking spot is about a dozen spaces closer to the District Courthouse than mine. Her Buick is already parked when I pull into the county complex. Rob's Mercedes is here too, just on the other side of the Buick. I am not surprised.

Last night's television coverage of the events leading up to my departure from Judge Gould's courtroom was painful to watch. But the coverage of Geraldine's performance during the motion to dismiss was far worse. Her campaign needs serious damage control. And I have hell to pay.

Harry argued brilliantly. Hour by hour, he accounted for Eddie Malone's whereabouts—and the state of his clothes and sneakers—

from the discovery of Skippy Eldridge's body through the moment of Eddie's arrest. In the end, he argued, there is only one explanation for the presence of Skippy's blood on Eddie's clothes and sneakers: somebody put it there.

There was a fatal flaw in Harry's argument and he knew it. That's why he expected to lose. But Geraldine, in her panic, failed to see it. The issues Harry argued to Judge Gould are factual, not legal. Questions of fact—no matter how obvious the answers may seem—should always be decided by a jury. The court shouldn't even consider a motion to dismiss unless it is based on a purely legal argument.

Instead of raising that rather rudimentary point, Geraldine stood mute after Harry's presentation. Confronted with the facts in the three affidavits for the first time, she simply had nothing to say. On the record, Harry's motion to dismiss stands unopposed. Judge Gould took the matter under advisement, saying he was "more than troubled" by the day's events. He promised a decision by the end of the week.

Rob and Geraldine are both in Rob's office with the door closed. A note on my chair in Rob's oversized scrawl tells me to buzz him when I arrive, but I am in no hurry to comply. Instead, I head to the lunchroom and pour a cup of coffee. I am not the only one in this office who has some explaining to do. I will meet with them when I am ready. And they will answer my questions first.

The door to Rob's office opens and, simultaneously it seems, Geraldine is behind me. She looks worse than I would have thought possible. Her eyes are bloodshot. The blond hair on top of her head is matted and flat, as if she wore a ski cap to bed last night.

But when I take in Geraldine's clothes, I realize she didn't go to bed last night. She's wearing the same suit and blouse she had on in the courtroom yesterday. Her makeup is dried out and cracked. She reeks of stale cigarette smoke. And she is livid. "I ought to fire you, Martha."

"If that's what you should do, Geraldine, go ahead and do it." The indifference in my own voice surprises me. The truth is that I can't get fired. I need access to my file cabinet when the police nab someone for Jake Junior's murder. That fact alone made me hesitate before heaving the file at Geraldine yesterday.

I am relieved, though I try hard not to show it, when Rob's words fill the lunchroom. "No one is getting fired over this, Geraldine."

Rob fills his own coffee mug, and directs me to his office with a wave of his hand. Geraldine is so close behind me I can actually hear her drag on her cigarette. Rob's office is literally filled with smoke, clouds of it drifting in the morning sunlight near the closed windows. Cigarette butts are everywhere. The general chaos in Rob's normally tidy office makes me realize that he and Geraldine have been here all night.

Rob points toward one of the chairs facing his desk, but I elect to stand. I open a window near his chair as high as it will go and lean against the sill. Rob sits down heavily, throws his glasses on top of the clutter on his desk, and leans on his elbows. "Marty, what's going on?"

For a fleeting moment I panic, imagining Rob and Geraldine have discovered the contents of the top drawer of my file cabinet. But that's impossible. The drawer is locked. The key is in my pocket, next to my Lady Smith. I decide to stick to the plan and take the offensive. "Why don't you tell me, Rob?"

An unexpected surge of anger rushes through me and I wheel around abruptly to face Geraldine. She actually jumps. "Better yet, why don't you tell me, Geraldine? Why don't you tell me why I walked into that courtroom yesterday—fully prepared to argue the motion—and got sent crawling back to my seat? That was quite an entrance you made, Geraldine. You were a female version of Clarence Darrow for a minute or two. So why don't you tell me what the hell is going on?"

Geraldine doesn't even blink. She walks to Rob's desk, picks up a copy of the Bridgewater report on Eddie Malone, and tosses it at me. "Page eight," she says.

I flip to page eight of the report, a log sheet of sorts. It details every departure Eddie Malone made from his hospital room during his twenty-day stay. The date and time of departure are in one narrow column. Eddie's destination is listed in the wide middle column. The time of return to his room is in the final narrow column.

Almost all of the entries reflect Eddie's trips to diagnostic therapy of one sort or another. But one is different. Halfway down the page is an entry that Geraldine has highlighted in yellow: *Fri. 6/11 @ 1025 hrs. / Conf. Rm. B—conf. w/ Attys Madigan and Nickerson / 1105 hrs.*

So that's it. Geraldine smells a rat. When she saw that I went to Bridgewater with Harry, and never mentioned that trip to her or to Rob, she concluded that Harry and I had forged some sort of an inappropriate alliance. She thought I would throw the competency hearing.

She is right, of course, about my alliance with Harry. But she couldn't be more wrong about the hearing. I still believe in the integrity of our criminal justice system. I still believe the system can—and does, in the long run, at least—work. I am well aware of the role I play in the system. So long as I continue to play that part, I will honor my oath of office.

I was prepared to argue against Harry's motion, to tell Judge Gould that the issues Harry raised are within the jury's province, not the judge's. I would have won, and the competency hearing would have gone forward. Harry knew that as well as I did. But Geraldine took over. She wasn't prepared to address the motion, and the competency hearing went nowhere. If Eddie Malone walks, it's on her shoulders, not mine.

I toss the report back on Rob's desk and direct my only comment to him. "So what?"

Rob puts his hands behind his head, his elbows pointed outward, and leans back in his chair. He is staring at me, assessing my candor. "Marty, you have to admit, it's highly unusual."

My fuse is uncharacteristically short this morning. I bark at him. "Highly unusual? Trying to get to the truth? Is that highly unusual? If it is, then we should all reread the oath we took when we were sworn in as prosecutors."

Reference to the oath sends Geraldine over the edge. She slams one open hand—the one not busy with the cigarette—down on Rob's desk. "Forget it, Martha. Your more-ethical-than-thou routine won't work this time. You're off homicide."

"I'm what?"

I turn to Rob. One look at him tells me he has already agreed to this. It took Geraldine all night to convince him, but in the end, she did.

Rob puts his face in his hands and Geraldine keeps talking. "You heard me. You're off homicide. An attorney who's running all over the Commonwealth with the goddamned Public Defender doesn't handle homicides in my office."

I keep my eyes on Rob. "This is still your office, Rob. Not Geraldine's. You have the final word here. What do you have to say?"

Rob lowers his hands, and I am sickened by the apology that is written on his face.

"Marty, you've been under a tremendous amount of stress in recent months. The Scott trial alone was a big burden, and you handled it beautifully. The subsequent murders in Chatham are weighing on all of us. But Jake Junior's death, that's been especially hard on you. Good God, an event like that would knock anyone down."

I don't move. I won't let him off that easily. He needs to say the words. After minutes of silence—Geraldine doesn't even inhale—Rob realizes why I'm waiting. At least he has the common decency to look me in the eyes.

"You're off homicide," he says.

CHAPTER 44

Thursday, June 24

Harry is waiting when I pull into my parking space, but he's not sitting on the curb. Instead, he is pacing the small patch of grass like a man whose wife is about to give birth in the parking lot. He hasn't shaved. His jacket and pants are both gray, but they don't match. I wonder if he knows.

He hands me a letter-sized envelope as soon as I join him on the grass. "Have you seen this yet?" he asks.

I haven't. The return address says it's from the Court of Appeals. I know without looking that it is the single justice's response to Harry's Rodriguez appeal.

The date stamp from the Public Defender's office indicates that Harry received the decision yesterday. My office probably did too. It must have gone to Geraldine. I feel slightly sick to my stomach as I digest the fact that the mail on homicides is no longer directed to my attention.

The envelope contains only two sheets of paper, so I know at once that Harry has lost on both counts. When a high court disagrees with a trial judge, it almost always feels compelled to explain its decision in detail. When a high court disagrees with a criminal defendant, it is less likely to do so. As a result, decisions reversing trial judges' rulings are usually lengthy and complete with citation to pertinent case law. Decisions affirming those rulings are more likely to be brief and conclusory.

Harry continues to pace while I stand still on the grass and read the opinion. Justice Russell Henderson disposes of the issues in little more than a page and a half. Most of his opinion is devoted to a recitation of the basic facts and a concise statement of the issues Harry raised in the two motions Judge Carroll denied. In the end, Justice Henderson rules:

The trial judge's failure to send the sequestered jurors back to their hotel rooms on the night of May 30 does not render the verdict unreliable. Although the jurors deliberated from eight o'clock on Sunday morning until approximately four o'clock on Monday morning—admittedly an unusually long day of deliberations—there is no evidence to suggest that any juror did so under duress. To the contrary, the record indicates that the judge's bailiff checked on the jurors repeatedly and, on each occasion, was informed by them that they wished to continue deliberations. The trial judge did not abuse his discretion in allowing them to do so.

Nor do I find any error in the trial judge's refusal to set aside the verdict after a similar murder was committed a year later in the same town. While such an occurrence may be unusual in the normally peaceful village of Chatham, I daresay it is routine in less privileged communities of the Commonwealth. The commission of a subsequent crime—even one with marked similarities—provides no basis upon which a trial judge should set aside a jury's verdict.

The decisions of the trial judge are affirmed. There is no need for a new trial, as there has been no miscarriage of justice.

Harry stops pacing when I stop reading.

"The problem is," I tell him, "that the subsequent murder did occur in the normally peaceful village of Chatham, not in one of the less privileged communities of the Commonwealth. To say that such an occurrence may be unusual in Chatham is the height of understatement."

"Bingo," he says. Harry has been shot down so many times in the appellate process that losing doesn't faze him anymore. "You're starting to sound like a defense lawyer," he tells me with a wink. "I like that."

It occurs to me that Justice Henderson's words are also the height of judicial indifference, but I don't say so. Enough sounding like a defense lawyer for one day.

Harry hands me yet another document, a new motion to dismiss the charges against Eddie Malone. It's the same motion he filed on behalf of Rodriguez, the same argument he just lost on appeal. This time, though, there is a third photograph added to the lineup, one of the shots I took of Jake Junior in the morgue. And once again, the whole motion, complete with photos, is copied to Woody Timmons at the *Cape Cod Times*.

If I am ever in trouble with the law, I want Harry on my side. He never gives up.

I hand the motion back to him. "You'll have to give that to Geraldine."

"Geraldine? Why Geraldine?"

"I'm off homicide, Harry."

He looks genuinely stricken. "Tell me you're joking, Marty."

"It's no joke. It's my punishment for running all over the Commonwealth with the Public Defender. And—though no one is saying so—for hanging Geraldine out to dry during Tuesday's motion."

Harry's stricken look disappears instantly. He raises his arms and his face to the cloudless sky. "Oh, sweet Jesus, that was golden. I'd sell my soul for a still shot of Geraldine's face when you walked out the courtroom door."

I can't help laughing, and when Harry laughs too, I laugh harder. Just like that, neither of us can stop. We stand in the county parking lot, Harry with his arms in the air, laughing until we both have tears in our eyes. Passersby either stare openly at us or keep their eyes glued to the ground, pretending we're not here. They might assume we're both scheduled for commitment proceedings.

I turn away from Harry to wipe my eyes, and my laughter comes to an abrupt halt. Geraldine's Buick is in her reserved spot. She is leaning against its driver's door, cigarette in hand. Her eyes are narrowed to slits.

CHAPTER 45

Friday, June 25

At five minutes before two I push my way through the back doors of the District Courtroom and slip down the left-hand aisle. I hope Geraldine won't notice me. She came to my office this morning to tell me I had already done enough damage in the Malone case. I was to stay away from the courtroom when Judge Gould rules on Harry's motion to dismiss, she said. Her prohibition only solidified my decision to attend. I probably would have been here anyway, but Geraldine's edict settled the matter.

I stop at the third bench from the front. It's already crowded, but Woody Timmons is on the end. He looks surprised to see me here, searching for a seat with the general public. He pushes his colleagues to the right, making room for me and my briefcase on the far left corner.

"Welcome to the wild side," he says.

The Kydd is at the counsel table with Geraldine, fidgeting with folders and documents. Geraldine, on the surface, looks more confident than she should. Rob is seated at the bar, and only those of us who know him well can see that he is worried. Eddie Malone is at the defense table with Harry, and Eddie just looks defeated.

Harry is the only person in the room who is genuinely enjoying himself. I can't help but feel just a little bit glad for him. By filing a motion he never expected to win, he somehow brought the District Attorney's office to its knees. A wonderful turn of events in the life of a public defender.

Judge Gould takes the bench promptly at two o'clock. Geraldine and Harry remain standing when the rest of us sit. Judge Gould ignores Geraldine. He delivers his decision to Harry and Eddie, as if they are the only two people in the room.

"Mr. Madigan, I have given your motion to dismiss the charges against Mr. Malone a great deal of thought. Technically, I should not have done so. You realize, I am sure, that the argument you make here depends entirely upon the resolution of factual questions. As such, it is an argument that should rightfully be presented to the jurors. I will not substitute my judgment for theirs."

I hold my breath as Geraldine turns forty-five degrees to her left. She doesn't look back far enough to notice me, though. Instead, she sets her lips in an almost imperceptible smile and telegraphs "I told you so" to Rob. My stomach tells me that's premature.

Judge Gould faces Geraldine while she is still turned away from him. He removes his glasses and folds them in his hands. He glares at her when she faces front again.

"I will, however, order that the District Attorney's office produce forthwith a complete and detailed report on the chain of custody of the evidence in this case. Furthermore, I order that the District Attorney's office do so for each and every piece of physical evidence it intends to offer against Edmund Malone."

The reporters stir, but they shouldn't. The defense is always entitled to chain-of-custody documentation for the Commonwealth's evidence. The rules of evidence require that any party who offers tangible items for admission at trial, such as the narcotics in a drug case or Eddie Malone's bloody clothes and sneakers in this case, must account for the whereabouts of those items from the moment they are seized from the defendant until the moment they are offered into evidence in the courtroom. It's unusual to be ordered to produce such documentation for every piece of evidence at this stage, but that is nothing more than an administrative burden. And it will fall on the Kydd's shoulders, not Geraldine's.

She gives the judge her most ingratiating smile. "The District Attorney's office will be happy to comply with the court's order, Your Honor."

She turns her frozen smile on Harry and takes her seat. But Judge Gould isn't through.

"That's not all you will comply with, Attorney Schilling."

There is an unmistakable edge in Judge Gould's voice. Geraldine undoubtedly hears it. She jumps back to her feet. The judge folds his arms on the bench and leans toward her.

"The court neither knows nor cares what your motivation was for the show you staged in this courtroom on Tuesday, Ms. Schilling."

Rob puts his face in his hands. The Kydd leans down toward the floor, fussing with papers in his briefcase. Geraldine grows pale and stares at the counsel table. Even I wince, involuntarily. Only Harry keeps his head held high as Judge Gould continues.

"But you won't get away with it again. This is a court of law, Ms. Schilling, no matter how many reporters are seated in the gallery. We don't pander to the press here. I will not stand by and watch you use the judicial system for political gain."

Rarely, if ever, has this courtroom been so quiet. But Judge Gould raises his voice anyway. "Any more grandstanding in this courtroom,

Ms. Schilling, and I will hold you in contempt. I mean that. I suggest you take this warning seriously."

If I were in Geraldine's shoes, I would assure the court that I take the warning seriously and sit down. It's pretty clear to me that Judge Gould is not in the mood to entertain explanations. Apparently, though, Geraldine reads the situation differently. She smiles at Judge Gould as if she understands the source of his confusion and is about to set him straight.

"Your Honor, perhaps I can explain." Geraldine moves away from the counsel table and takes a few steps toward the bench. Judge Gould sits back in his chair, expressionless. It occurs to me that he might allow her to take just enough rope to hang herself.

"I am sure Your Honor is familiar with Attorney Martha Nickerson of our office."

I bolt upright at the mention of my name. So does the Kydd. Woody Timmons turns sideways to stare at me. I keep my eyes focused forward, but I am certain he can just about read my thoughts. Judge Gould leans forward in his chair again and nods at Geraldine, but says nothing.

"Your Honor is aware, then, that Ms. Nickerson has served our office well for many years."

Woody is gaping at me, unabashed. He knows as well as I do that Geraldine is not standing before the court to praise my career as an Assistant District Attorney. She is setting the stage to pass the buck. Somehow, she is going to blame Tuesday's fiasco on me.

"But lately, Your Honor, the stress of working homicide has taken its toll on Ms. Nickerson. Your Honor may not be aware that the homicide victim found in Chatham on June fourteenth was a personal friend of Ms. Nickerson's. Her son's high school teammate. The son of two of her own former schoolmates. Such an event would take a toll on any human being, Your Honor."

Judge Gould puts his glasses on again, his expression stern. "And your point, Ms. Schilling?"

"Well, Your Honor, I certainly don't want to disparage Attorney Nickerson. That's not my intention at all. I will only say that just before Tuesday's hearing, it came to my attention that Attorney Nickerson had engaged in some questionable conduct during her investigation of the Malone case."

The reporters buzz. Judge Gould bangs his gavel only once, hard. They fall silent. Harry wheels his chair around and stares openly at Geraldine. She is unmoved by his scrutiny.

"In any event, Your Honor, it became clear to me that Ms. Nickerson would not zealously represent the interests of the Commonwealth at Tuesday's hearing, as is her duty. I had no choice but to intervene."

My cheeks are burning, but I don't care. I have zealously represented the interests of the Commonwealth of Massachusetts each and every day since I took the oath. Tuesday was no exception, and I want that fact on the record. I stand up to address the court from my spot on the end of the third row. "That's not true, Your Honor. That's simply not true."

This time Judge Gould's gavel has little impact on the swell of noise from the gallery. Everyone in the room, it seems, is standing and shouting. I am momentarily blinded by the glare of dozens of flashbulbs. When my vision clears, Judge Gould is standing behind his raised bench, fuming.

"Ms. Schilling, Ms. Nickerson, Mr. Madigan," he bellows. "In my chambers. Now."

CHAPTER 46

At eleven o'clock, I collapse into the overstuffed chair that faces the sofa in our small, pine-paneled living room. With my back to the television, I watch Luke watch the news. I wonder how he feels when he sees his mother and father on the air night after night, embroiled in separate, but equally ugly, proceedings. I wonder how he responds when his friends ask questions about our cases. I wonder how he will look back on all of this when he reaches adulthood.

I watch Luke closely when the news station airs Geraldine's accusation against me along with my protest from the gallery. I watch him as I listen to my own words, my voice sounding surprisingly authoritative, not like my voice at all: "That's not true, Your Honor. That's simply not true."

Luke actually stands up and claps, laughing. "Way to go, Mom. Don't let Geraldine push you around."

I didn't. In the minute it took to walk from the gallery to Judge Gould's chambers, I made an important decision. I decided to trust my instincts. I decided to do what I ask every potential juror to do before every trial—trust my gut. And my gut told me that Geraldine was offering me up as a sacrificial lamb. She was willing to end my career, if necessary, in order to further hers. That didn't sit well with me.

When we entered chambers, I walked straight to the judge's desk and opened my briefcase on top of it. I took out my copy of Harry's emergency motion and handed it to Judge Gould. Geraldine started talking at once, of course, but the judge silenced her with one forbidding stare. He took his time looking over my copy of the motion, complete with handwritten notes and case citations in the margins, while the rest of us stood in silence. Then, without looking at any of us, he buzzed his courtroom clerk and asked her to send in the stenographer.

Judge Gould continued to ignore all of us, looking only at the stenographer, as he sat down behind his desk and began dictating. First he summarized Tuesday's events, reciting in excruciatingly painful detail Geraldine's grand entrance—"highly disruptive and self-serving," he called it—and her subsequent floundering, her inability to offer any response to Harry's motion.

Next the judge summarized today's events, directing the court reporter to quote Geraldine's exact words when she accused me of questionable conduct, when she claimed I would have failed to zealously represent the interests of the Commonwealth at Tuesday's hearing.

Finally, Judge Gould swiveled in his chair and looked steadily at each of us in turn—Harry, me, and at last, Geraldine. His eyes remained fixed on hers as he finished dictating. "It is not Attorney Nickerson's conduct that this court finds questionable. To the contrary, Attorney Nickerson's handwritten notes made in preparation for the motion were thorough and persuasive. The result she espoused—or would have espoused had she not been silenced by Attorney Schilling—was precisely the result reached by this court on its own volition. The cases she cited—or would have cited had she been permitted to do so—were appropriate.

"Attorney Schilling's conduct, on the other hand, was questionable at best. Not only on Tuesday, but today as well. Through the eyes of this court, it appears that Attorney Schilling, having regrets over her misguided performance on Tuesday, sought today to lay the blame for her poor judgment on the shoulders of her subordinate."

Judge Gould stood, then, and leaned forward over his desk, keeping his eyes on Geraldine's, their faces only inches apart. He pointed at her the way I pointed at Manuel Rodriguez a month ago. "If that is true, Attorney Schilling, shame on you."

The last vestige of color drained from Geraldine's face. She looked as though she would like to faint, if at all possible. When Judge Gould concluded, I thought she just might.

"This court has neither the time nor the resources to get to the bottom of this matter. But get to the bottom of it we will. I hereby order that a copy of this transcript, along with all supporting documentation, be forwarded to the Board of Bar Overseers. I direct that a formal inquiry be conducted into the allegations that have been made here."

Judge Gould's eyes were glued to Geraldine's. "I direct the Board to determine whether or not Attorney Schilling made false statements to this court, and whether or not she abused the powers of her office."

CHAPTER 47

Saturday, June 26

Last night's news coverage gave Geraldine a black eye. It annihilated Ralph.

It seems Ralph testified that he knew about his patient's ties to Lester Pan. He knew, also, that Lester Pan was paying the freight for his services. The prosecutor predictably pointed out that Ralph had failed to mention that fact during his earlier testimony, hadn't he? Ralph should have just said yes. What he said instead was ill-advised.

"You didn't ask," he responded.

As a prosecutor, I am always pleased when an adverse witness gives me that answer. If the witness happens to be an expert, I am delighted. When cross-examining expert witnesses, I deliberately save my "You didn't mention . . . , did you?" questions until the very end. If I am lucky enough to hear the expert tell me it was because I didn't ask, I immediately announce that I have no further questions and sit down. I have all I need, at that point, to destroy that witness's credibility during closing argument.

It was obvious from last night's footage that the prosecutor cross-examining Ralph shares my view of the "you didn't ask" answer. When Ralph uttered his unfortunate reply, the prosecutor looked jubilant. He arched his eyebrows at the judge, lifted his hands in the air as if he'd just scored a touchdown, and said, "That's all I have, Your Honor." Ralph looked sick.

And on that note, the King County Superior Court in Seattle adjourned for the week. Closing arguments will begin Monday morning. When the prosecuting attorney gets his turn, Ralph will be verbally drawn and quartered. And Ralph has been through enough trials to know that's exactly what's coming.

I have to give him credit, though. He made the long trip and he's here to take Luke to the Red Sox game Luke gave him for Father's Day. And as fate would have it, the Sox are playing the Seattle Mariners. Too bad for Ralph. On this particular weekend, he would probably prefer to avoid all reminders of Seattle.

The game doesn't start until seven, so Luke will spend tonight in Boston with Ralph. Tomorrow, they will celebrate Luke's seventeenth birthday by visiting Boston's downtown attractions—Faneuil Hall, Quincy Market, the Swan Boats, and Boston Harbor. Ralph seems to be catching on to the fact that our son is happiest outdoors.

Luke's birthday is actually next weekend, but he will be busy then, celebrating with his friends at the annual beach bonfire at Justin's, an event Ralph wants no part of. And Ralph will be out of town next weekend anyway. He's been retained by yet another wealthy accused murderer, this one a stockbroker in Cincinnati who allegedly felt he needed the proceeds from his wife's life insurance policy sooner rather than later.

Ralph arrives at three o'clock, as scheduled. He looks worse today than he did on television last night. And I don't think the six-hour flight from Seattle is to blame. There is something about watching one's own courtroom performance on the television news—particularly when the proceedings didn't go well from your perspective—that saps every last ounce of energy from the soul. Ralph would never believe it, but I feel sorry for him.

Luke is packed and ready to go. Danny Boy follows him to the BMW, whimpering all the way. As always, I wave until they are out of sight.

I am somewhat surprised to realize that I am pleased. After all these years—after the anger, the pain, the life-altering disappointment—I'm happy that Luke and Ralph are finally finding each other.

CHAPTER 48

Monday, June 28

Geraldine hasn't spoken to me since Friday's hearing. Not a word. I passed her in the hallway when she arrived this morning, and she looked right through me. A month ago—two weeks ago, even—I would have been thrown by that. Today I feel nothing but indifference.

The District Court docket was heavy this morning, no surprise on a summer Monday. I volunteered to handle it alone, freeing the Kydd to tend to his many assignments on the Skippy Eldridge and Jake Junior murders. He was grateful for the time, and I was glad to keep busy. Now that I'm finished—at three o'clock—I have nothing else to do.

Geraldine is barricaded in her office. She's been in there all day, preparing to defend herself before the Board of Bar Overseers, preparing to say whatever needs to be said to get her campaign back on track. Rob's office door is open when I walk by, and I am barely seated before he appears in my office and closes the door.

"Marty," he says, "the Board has scheduled its initial hearing on Geraldine's matter. A week from today. Nine o'clock."

I nod at him, but say nothing.

"You're on the witness list," he says. "In fact, you're scheduled to testify first, before anyone else. You're going to have a big impact on this thing, Marty. You should give some thought to the content of your testimony."

There it is again—a feeling that was foreign to me until recently—indifference.

"I intend to tell the truth, Rob. No dress rehearsal necessary."

Rob studies me carefully for a couple of minutes. He parts his lips to speak, but apparently decides against it. He says nothing more before he retreats, leaving my office door open behind him.

Alone in my office, I wonder if Rob got a glimpse of the change in me that I am just beginning to see in myself. It is a change I have not yet fully acknowledged, even to myself. It's not so much that I feel betrayed by my office. After all, I betrayed my office first, when I agreed to plant the surveillance equipment with Harry and Bobo, when I agreed to spy on my own coworkers. It's bigger than that.

I realize—as I sit in my office with nothing to do—that I feel betrayed by the criminal justice system. It's not what it claims to be, not what it should be. I am part of it, but I can't make it work. There is no avenue available to deal properly with the events of the past month. Harry has traveled every possible path, and they all lead nowhere.

My thoughts are interrupted by a timid knock on my open office door. It's Charlie Cahoon.

"Miss Marty, is this a bad time? Did I come at a bad time?"

It's the first time I've seen Charlie out of his house since we buried Jake Junior. I stop by most evenings, on my way home from work, and try to coax him over to the cottage to have dinner with Luke and me, but he always refuses.

"Not at all, Charlie. Come in. Sit down."

Charlie takes a seat, but he doesn't look comfortable. I stand and cross the room to close the door behind him. I lean against the edge of my desk, near his chair, instead of returning to my own seat.

"How are you, Charlie?"

"Well, Miss Marty, I'm all right. I'm sorry to barge in like this . . ."

"You're not barging in, Charlie. You know I'm always happy to see you. You want some coffee?"

"No. No, thank you. What I want is an honest answer."

I have known that this moment would come since the day Jake Junior died. I managed to postpone it the day after, when Charlie wondered aloud about Harry's representations to the court the day he ended up in jail. I have known all along that the question would resurface. And I've agonized over how I should handle it. I have struggled to understand how much suffering Charlie—or any human spirit, for that matter—can endure.

"Miss Marty, there's something I have to ask you." Charlie is turning his hat around and around in his hands. "In the newspapers, they say . . . well, especially that *Times* reporter, that Timmons fellow, he says . . ."

There are tears in Charlie's eyes, and I can't bear to watch him struggle any longer. "I know, Charlie, I know what he says."

Charlie blinks back his tears and looks straight into my eyes. "Is it true, Miss Marty? Do you even know if it's true? If you don't, I'll have to ask Dr. Skinner. He must know. But I don't know him too well, and I thought if you knew . . ."

I have to answer him. Jeff's response to Charlie's question would almost certainly be sterile, a clinician's view of the lacerations on the corpse. Charlie deserves better.

I open my mouth to tell him, but no sound comes out.

"Miss Marty, please tell me. Did you see Jake Junior after he died? Did you see . . . did you see his chest?"

I lean down and look into Charlie's pained eyes and just like that, it's clear to me. Charlie wants the truth, and he is entitled to it, even if it hurts like hell.

"I saw him, Charlie. I saw him in the morgue. I even took photographs."

I stand up straight and hold my head in my hands for just a second before looking back at him. "It's true, Charlie. Woody Timmons is reporting the truth. Jake Junior was labeled with a Roman numeral three."

Charlie sits completely still. He seems to shrink in his chair. But the pain in his eyes expands.

CHAPTER 49

Being idle is far more tiring than being busy. By five o'clock, I am exhausted. Geraldine is still barricaded, and Rob and the Kydd are both at their desks when I check the lock on my file cabinet, grab my briefcase, and head out the office door. From the lobby, I see a dozen reporters camped on the front steps of the District Courthouse.

I take the side exit, but Woody Timmons spots me almost immediately. "Attorney Nickerson," he calls out. "Has there been a break in the Cahoon investigation? Is an arrest imminent?"

The questions take me by surprise. Given my present status in the office, I can't help but wonder if Woody Timmons knows something I don't. "No. No break at all. Why do you ask?"

They are crowding around me now, too many of them between me and the Thunderbird. Microphones are outstretched and cameras are rolling, but Woody is the only one talking. He seems to be their appointed ambassador.

"We've been told the victim's grandfather was here today. In your office, as a matter of fact. That led to speculation that there may have been some development in the investigation."

A week ago, I would have ignored all of them, even Woody Timmons. I would have told him to speak to Rob, or to Geraldine. I would have refused to answer even the simplest of questions. I would have pushed past all of them and locked myself in the Thunderbird.

But not today. Today I am grateful. At least Woody Timmons appears interested in getting to the truth. "No," I tell him. "Nothing yet."

I lower my head and move toward the Thunderbird, but Woody isn't finished. "Ms. Nickerson," he says, "we've never heard from you on the subject of Roman numerals. Your boss says there aren't any. What do you say?"

I am startled when I look up. Woody Timmons is standing uncomfortably close to me, his face just inches from mine. I have no alternative but to look him straight in the eyes and when I do, I understand that my answer is important. I also understand that if Charlie Cahoon must bear the gut-wrenching pain of the truth, then the rest of us must do so as well.

I set my briefcase down on the black tarmac of the parking lot and return Woody's stare. The other reporters fade into the background. I realize that my decision is already made. I just have to go through with it.

"Sometimes," I tell him, "the truth is so ugly we can't bring ourselves to look at it. We hide from it. But we can only hide temporarily. Eventually, we have to face it. There's really no alternative."

The parking lot falls eerily silent.

"The truth is that Michael Scott's wounds looked like a Roman numeral one the first time I saw them. I didn't think much about it, and I didn't mention it at the trial. My mistake."

The other reporters stir, but Woody Timmons doesn't move a muscle.

"There is no doubt in my mind that a Roman numeral two was etched into Skippy Eldridge. My superiors say it isn't so. But if it is so, they say, it's nothing more than a copycat sequel to the Scott murder. I wanted that to be the fact. I chose to believe it. Again, my mistake."

I have a sense of the crowd around me growing louder, but I keep my focus on Woody.

"And Jake Cahoon was branded with a Roman numeral three. My superiors still say it isn't so. But I've made two mistakes already. I won't make a third, if I can help it."

Woody Timmons nods at me, a grateful look on his face. He is relieved, I know, to have company out on the public limb that he and Harry have occupied alone until now. For the first time, I take my eyes from his face and address the other reporters. I can't really see them; there are too many bright lights in my eyes, too many flash-bulbs exploding.

"Someone is murdering young men on the shores of Chatham and numbering their corpses. We will never stop him if we don't face the fact that he's out there. Please, call on the District Attorney's office to treat these cases as serial murders, and to take all available steps to prevent the next one. Don't wait for number four."

I pick up my briefcase and head for the car. I probably just lost my job. But I had to do it. I have to do all that I can do.

Chapter 50

Wednesday, June 30

Barnstable County employees get paid on the last business day of every month, always at the end of the day. Sheila O'Brien from the accounting office wheels a metal cart—a smaller version of the ones used in grocery stores—through the complex, delivering one sealed gray envelope to each employee, the employee's full name showing through the window in front. This monthly task has fallen to Sheila for twenty years, since she arrived on Cape Cod straight from County Cork in Ireland. And she is highly skilled at handling the good-natured abuse that comes her way as a result.

Every payday the Kydd props the door to our offices open so he can listen to the banter. Since I have nothing better to do on this particular payday—even the regular docket was light this morning—I saunter down the hall to join him. He is already grinning when I get there.

"Hey, Sheila," someone hollers from the mail room, "you forgot a zero on this check—and the decimal point is all wrong."

"Is that so?" Sheila responds calmly, her normally light brogue growing a bit thick. "Well, then, we'll have to settle up next month, won't we? Just think of it as money in the bank. A nest egg of sorts."

And it's not just the mail room staffers who deem themselves underpaid. Even the Chief Civil Clerk feels less than appreciated. "Now, Sheila," she calls from her office. "Why don't you keep this check and buy the governor a nice cup of coffee?"

Sheila doesn't miss a beat. "I would, dear," she sings back, "but the governor likes a wee bun with his coffee and that check would never suffice."

The Kydd is laughing out loud by the time Sheila wheels her cart into our section. She disappears into Rob's office first, then Geraldine's. The Kydd's office is next in line and, as usual, Sheila delivers a piece of advice along with his paycheck. "Don't get wild and crazy with all that money, lad. Soon you'll have a bride to support, you know."

Sheila has what seems to be an endless supply of nieces in the Old Country, any one of which, according to Sheila, would make an ideal wife for the Kydd. She's been trying to marry him off since he got here. One of her favorite candidates, niece Cara, her brother's eldest, is staying with Sheila for the summer, working two waitress jobs. The Kydd has agreed to take her out this Saturday night. I can't be certain, but I think he's dreading it.

"Okay, Sheila," he says. "I'm saving. I'm saving."

Sheila gives the Kydd a skeptical look, as if they are in-laws already, and drops his paycheck on the blotter in front of him. When she hands me mine, she tosses her black curls back toward Geraldine's office. "Where's the Queen Bee?"

Sheila calls Geraldine the Queen Bee only when Geraldine can't hear her. I raise my finger to my lips to silence her and lower my voice to a whisper. "She's in her office, isn't she?"

"Do you think I've lost my marbles, Marty? Of course she's not in her office. Her briefcase is gone. The light's out."

The Kydd nods to confirm Sheila's account. "She's gone for the day, Marty. Left about an hour ago."

It's odd for Geraldine to leave the office early. She arrives late sometimes, but she almost never leaves early. I raise my eyebrows at the Kydd, but he shrugs. "Don't look at me," he says. "I'm just a drone. The queen doesn't tell me what's going on."

With that, Sheila resumes her rounds, heading toward the probation officers, by far her toughest customers, she says. I walk slowly back to my office, my sealed gray envelope in hand, wondering what I will do with myself when I get there.

When I reach my desk, I open the envelope and tuck the check into my jacket pocket. I am about to toss the envelope into the trash can when I realize it's not empty. It holds another sheet of paper, the same size as the check. It's pink.

I know at once that I am holding the reason for Geraldine's early departure. She is, I realize for the first time, a coward. She didn't want to be here—didn't want to face me—when I received this:

Notice of Change of Status
Employee: Martha Nickerson
Former status: Active
Present Status: Administrative Leave—Paid
Instructions: Remove all personal items from office by close of business today. Do not return to premises unless so directed in writing.

It's the last line—the signature line—that hurts. The form is signed by Rob Mendell.

CHAPTER 51

Thursday, July 1

The Kydd is not the least bit surprised. I expect him to be shocked—horrified, even—when I tell him about the cameras and microphones hidden in the evidence room and the holding cells. Instead, he nods calmly, looking from Harry to me, silently absorbing the information we're giving him, the unbelievable request we're making of him. For a long time, he says nothing.

I am racked with guilt. Three times in the past hour, I have told the Kydd what he already knows. If he helps us, he almost certainly forfeits his future with the District Attorney's office. If he doesn't help us, another young man in Chatham will probably die.

We are seated at my kitchen table. The Kydd came here straight from work, just as I asked. Harry has been here all afternoon, agonizing over this decision with me. But in fact, we both knew all along that we had no alternative. When the time comes, when the cops bag some punk for Jake Junior's murder, someone has to monitor the surveillance equipment in my office. And, on weekdays at least, I no longer have access to it.

The Kydd shakes his head up and down and takes a deep breath. "Okay," he says. "I'll do it."

I reach into my pocket for the key to my wooden file cabinet, but Harry gives me a look that stops me. He leans across the table toward the Kydd. "Make sure," he says. "Don't say yes unless you're sure."

The Kydd looks back at Harry without blinking. "I don't know you too well, Mr. Madigan. But I think I've gotten to know Marty pretty well during the past year. If she says those three corpses were numbered, then I believe they were. And that means I really don't have a choice."

The Kydd looks from Harry to me. "I'm sure," he says. "I'm with you."

I take the key from my pocket and drop it into his outstretched hand. He stares at it for a moment, and gives me a small grin. "Top drawer, right?"

I am stunned. "How did you know?"

His grin expands. "Your files," he says. "They appeared in my file cabinet last Monday."

The files. I completely forgot. I moved them the day Bobo installed the equipment, but never said a word to the Kydd about them.

The Kydd is grinning broadly now. "The cases are Adams to Bergman," he says. "That's the top drawer."

Harry finds this hilarious. "You're good, Kydd," he says through his laughter. "I have to hand it to you. You're good. What else have you noticed that you haven't mentioned?"

I don't think Harry expects an answer to his question, but the Kydd appears to have one. Harry stops laughing as soon as he realizes.

"Well, actually," the Kydd says, "there is something."

Harry leans farther across the table, all traces of laughter gone. "What is it, Kydd? Tell us."

The Kydd is hesitant. He gives us both a nervous grin. "It's just a thought," he says. "It's just a thought about the dates."

Harry nods at him.

"I think the dates might matter, all three of them," the Kydd says. He swallows hard before he elaborates. "If you look into the origin of Memorial Day, you'll find that General John Alexander Logan ordered that the graves of all military men killed during the American Civil War be decorated on May thirtieth, 1868. That was the first Memorial Day."

Harry and I are silent. The Kydd continues, self-consciously. "Only they didn't call it that."

The Kydd looks at me, inviting the question.

"What did they call it, Kydd?"

He swallows again. "They called it Decoration Day."

A chill runs down my spine. Harry leans back in his chair and lets out a low whistle.

"But Jake Junior," I say to the Kydd. "He wasn't killed on Memorial Day. What about him?"

"Jake Junior was murdered on June fourteenth," he begins.

"Another Monday," I say.

The Kydd shakes his head. "Not just another Monday," he says. "Flag Day."

Harry jumps out of his chair. I am glued to mine. "Flag Day," I repeat. "Why does that matter?"

The Kydd looks across the table at Harry, and I can see that they are on the same page. Harry takes over. "Our killer just happens to be operating in Chatham, Marty. But he's mad as hell at the whole god-damned country. On two consecutive Decoration Days, he decorated a corpse. After the second one, he couldn't wait that long to do it again. So he decorated the third corpse on Flag Day."

Harry sits down again, runs both hands through his tangled hair, and takes a deep breath. "He's not going to be able to wait very long this time either. He'll need to decorate a fourth corpse sometime soon."

Harry nods at the Kydd, then looks me straight in the eyes. "And we're just hours away from the Fourth of July, Marty. America's Birthday."

CHAPTER 52

≡

Saturday, July 3

Being at Rob's house is awkward, to say the least. The trust between us is gone. But Luke and Justin have celebrated their birthdays together for years, and Rob and I agreed that "our situation"—as he calls it—shouldn't ruin the boys' plans. Even so, I do my best to avoid conversation with him. When Jeff wanders in from next door, he gives me a comforting hug. The word has gotten around. I leave him and Rob in the kitchen—molding hamburger patties—and head out to Rob's oceanside deck.

I fire up the charcoal grill and appoint myself head chef. Jeff brings me a glass of white wine along with two trays of raw hamburgers and hot dogs from the kitchen. He sips his own glass of wine on the deck while I flip burgers and dogs on the grill and the party guests play volleyball on the beach. As they rotate in and out of the game, small groups of Luke's friends follow their noses to the grill for dinner. The girls are content after one round of sandwiches, but the boys, it seems, will never stop eating.

Luke didn't want to come here tonight. Not so much because of the awkwardness with Rob—I haven't given Luke the ugly details—but because of what happened to Jake Junior. It doesn't seem right, Luke said, to have a party so soon. If Jake Junior were here, I asked him, what would he want you to do?

Luke didn't answer, but he's here. And for the first time since Jake Junior died, Luke is wearing the army tee shirt Jake Junior gave to him and the rest of the team. It's Luke's small way, I think, of inviting Jake Junior's spirit to the party. Do all that you can do. Be all that you can be.

And I am glad that Luke is here. These thirty-eight kids have gone through eleven years of school and life together. They are a tight-knit group. They share a bond that only a small-town childhood can create. And every one of them has been touched in some way by the two most recent murders. It's good for them to be together, to celebrate, to try to forget.

It's especially good for Luke and Justin. They are the best of friends, and they lean on each other through all of life's peaks and valleys. They have confided in each other completely since Jake Junior's death, spending hours walking the beaches of the Monomoy Wildlife Refuge and talking. Luke will spend the night here tonight, in Justin's top bunk, as he does every year.

I was reluctant to let Luke spend the night at Justin's this year. No Chatham beach feels safe anymore. My instinct is to keep Luke close, but I can't let fear take over his life—or mine. Fear destroys.

Luke, of course, laughed at my concern. "We live on the beach too," he said.

"True," I admitted.

"And Rob Mendell's security system is state of the art."

"Also true."

He laughed. "Ours is Danny Boy."

"Good point. Go pack."

When they wake up tomorrow, Luke and Justin will both be seventeen, headed into their senior year at Chatham High School. It's hard for me to believe. Just yesterday, it seems, they were nervous first-graders.

Dinner is over. The sky is turning brilliant shades of pink and purple, and the sun is dropping, inch by inch, into Nantucket Sound. The kids have already built the traditional bonfire—a pile of driftwood taller than they are. The sun's descent is their cue to light it. Jeff hangs around just long enough to see the pyre ignite, then waves good night to Rob and me and heads back to the serenity next door.

Justin and Rob run back and forth to the kitchen and, like the loaves and fishes, an endless supply of graham crackers, Hershey bars, and marshmallows miraculously appears. The kids settle into small groups around the fire, talking, laughing, and roasting s'mores. Luke seems happy.

I help Rob with cleanup and bid him good night. He is relieved to see me go, I know. He is more uncomfortable about "our situation" than I am. Too bad, I think, that Geraldine has such complete control over the office.

It's almost midnight when I pull up to the cottage, and I hear the telephone ringing from the driveway. I hurry through the back door and trip over Danny Boy; he doesn't move very quickly anymore. I tell him I'm sorry, flip on the kitchen light, and grab the cordless from the counter.

It's Harry. "Marty," he says, "turn on the news."

The news is normally over by eleven-thirty, but I don't argue. I carry the phone with me into the living room and turn on the television. A banner at the top of the screen tells me I am watching live footage of breaking news. Regularly scheduled programming, it says, will resume when coverage is complete.

The live image of the television news anchor gives way to previously recorded footage of a leather-clad male, his black coat covering his face, being corralled through the side door of the District Courthouse by a dozen Barnstable police officers, all with weapons drawn. Everyone on the screen is soaking wet, even the guy in leather.

Harry identifies the soggy male under the leather coat before the anchor does. "It's Angel," he says.

Angelo Santini is known as "Angel" on the streets, a misnomer of the highest order. Angel is anything but. He makes Manuel Rodriguez look like an altar boy. According to the television anchorman, who is now a talking head in the corner of the screen, Angel was arrested in Hyannis approximately two hours ago and charged with a dozen offenses, at least half of them felonies.

Angel had been in custody for about an hour, the talking head says, when he was moved from the police station to the holding cells at the Barnstable District Courthouse. Shortly after that, the charges against him were amended. Just moments ago, First Assistant District Attorney Geraldine Schilling confirmed by telephone that Angelo Santini is now charged with the first-degree murder of Jacob Cahoon, Jr.

The phone is plastered to the side of my head. "Saturday night," I hear myself saying into the receiver. "He won't be arraigned until Tuesday; Monday's a holiday."

"Between now and then," Harry says, "our guy will gin up some evidence. And if he's planning to commemorate the Fourth of July, he's going to have a busy weekend."

"I still have my keys to the courthouse, Harry. I'm on my way."

I keep the radio news on during the drive to Barnstable, but the reports don't add any new information about Angel. There is, though, late breaking news on the West Coast. The Dr. Wu jury, having begun deliberations on Tuesday morning, came back with its verdict just moments ago. After four full days of deliberating, the panel rejected the insanity defense completely. On five independent counts of first-degree murder, the jury found Willie Chung guilty as charged.

I'm glad Ralph is in Cincinnati.

It's one o'clock when I park behind the courthouse, at the far end of a half-dozen Barnstable County vans. It's better, I think, to park away from my regular spot and the parking lot lights.

Harry is already here, waiting in the darkness by the side door.

CHAPTER 53

Sunday, July 4

My key doesn't work. I should have known. Geraldine undoubtedly realized I didn't turn it in. She had the lock changed.

Harry uses his cell phone to call the Kydd, but he gets the answering machine. Three times he urges the Kydd to pick up, to no avail, then leaves his number and snaps the phone shut. "Where the hell is he?"

Harry doesn't expect me to know the answer to that question, but I do. "He's out with Cara O'Brien."

"With who?"

"Cara O'Brien, Sheila O'Brien's niece. She's visiting for the summer from Ireland. Sheila's been pestering the Kydd since Cara got here. He finally agreed to take her out—and tonight's the night."

"Who the hell is Sheila O'Brien?"

Harry is moving me toward his Wrangler before I answer. "She works in accounting," I tell him.

"Marty, I don't give a damn where she works. Where does she live?"

"In Yarmouth. You drive. I think I can find it."

The town of Yarmouth is east of Barnstable, and in twenty minutes, we are on Sheila's street. Her house is easy to find; her car is in the driveway and her name is on the mailbox, a single green shamrock next to it. The porch light is on. Harry bangs hard on the screen door and Sheila answers just a minute or so later in her bathrobe. "Glory be to God," she says, "there's trouble."

I push Harry to the side and open the door. "Sheila, Cara is fine. The Kydd is fine. But we need to find him. Fast. I don't have time to explain. When do you expect them back?"

"I'm sure I don't know, Marty. They didn't get going until after nine. Cara, the poor thing, had to work later than expected. They went to a movie, then planned to stop for a bite to eat."

"What movie? When did it start?"

My tone is making Sheila nervous. She fingers the lapel of her terry-cloth robe. "Something in Dennis," she says. "I don't recall the title; nothing I would enjoy. It started at ten-fifteen."

I hold my watch under Sheila's porch lamp. One-thirty. The movie's over. "Any clue where they went to eat?"

I am beginning to feel desperate, and the look on Sheila's face tells me it shows. "Now, there I can help, Marty. Cara's been aching to have dinner at Claude's since the first time she laid eyes on the place. And I've mentioned that fact to the Kydd more than once. I'll bet the farm that's where he's taken her."

Claude's Restaurant is at the mouth of Bass River, another twenty minutes south of here. Harry hands Sheila a business card with his cell phone number circled. "Everything closes at two," he tells her. "If you see him before we do, have him call that number. It's important."

"I'll do that," she says, turning her worried face toward me. "You be careful, Marty. I'll say a wee prayer."

"Oh no, Sheila," I tell her. "Better make it a whopper."

CHAPTER 54

Cara O'Brien is drop-dead gorgeous, with a luminous complexion and jet black hair cascading to her waist. She and the Kydd are seated at a candlelit table in the window, having after-dinner brandy. Harry stops the Wrangler right in front of their window, beside the front door, but the Kydd is captivated. He wouldn't notice if the building fell down around him.

Harry leaves the engine running. From the passenger seat, I see him barge past the hostess without explanation and appear in the window with Cara and the Kydd. The Kydd jumps to his feet, removes his car key from his key ring, and hands it to Cara. Seconds later, he is in the back seat of the Wrangler and we are speeding through back roads toward the Barnstable District Courthouse.

The new lock, the Kydd tells us during the drive, was not supposed to be installed until next week. Geraldine gave him a new key on Friday afternoon, along with the new alarm code, but said neither would be needed until Tuesday, at the earliest, since Monday is a holiday. He put the key on his ring so he wouldn't lose it. He planned to have copies made for Harry and me this weekend.

By the time we reach the courthouse, it's almost three o'clock, almost four hours since Angel was brought here. The Kydd unlocks the door easily. Harry and I both stand back while he enters the new code to disarm the security system. I am stung by how quickly I have become an outsider.

The Kydd and Harry head downstairs while I unlock my office, grateful that one of my keys still works. We agreed, while driving here, that I would surf the channels to find out which cell Angel is in, rewind the film in that camera by four hours or so, and find out if we missed anything. In the meantime, Harry will head down to the cells. He has defended Angel in the past, and will claim to be on hand to represent him this time, should Angel so choose.

Harry will identify the officers on guard duty, engage them in conversation, if possible. At the same time, the Kydd will scope out the evidence room. He is the only one of the three of us who can claim a legitimate reason to be there, though I can't imagine what that reason would be during the small hours of Sunday morning.

I find Angel on the second try. I assumed they would put him on one end or the other, and they did. Angel is in cell six, at the far end of the corridor. When I tune in to channel seven, I have a clear view of Angel, from overhead, on the cot in his prison-issued orange jumpsuit. He's asleep.

The Kydd is back in my office even before I finish rewinding four hours' worth of film. The evidence room is quiet, he reports. No one is there. The door is locked and the lights are out. He leaves and returns seconds later with two counter stools from the lunchroom. We sit side by side in front of the cabinet as the film whirls backward, taking us four hours back in time in cell six.

Harry returns from his trip downstairs with a wealth of information. Sergeants Sharkey and Kane—both seasoned veterans of the Barnstable Police Department—are seated in the dim hallway, guns in their holsters, their prisoner asleep. They told Harry all they knew about the arrest.

It was a routine traffic stop, they said. Or at least it started that way. Angel ran a red light in the middle of Hyannis with an unmarked cruiser three cars behind. When the officer turned on the blue lights, Angel took off.

A high-speed chase ensued, ending when Angel lost control of his car, knocked over a fire hydrant, and careened to a stop against the brick wall behind it. The hydrant rolled into the street, and a twenty-foot plume of water shot into the air. Six Barnstable squad cars called in to assist formed a semicircle around Angel's car. He refused to get out. The water, he told them, would ruin his new outfit. By the time they extricated him, everybody was drenched.

Angel was charged with everything from driving to endanger to destruction of public property to resisting arrest, and transported to the Barnstable police station for processing. He was not charged with murder; not then, anyway. His car was impounded and, per standard police procedure, an inventory search was conducted.

The inventory search is, perhaps, law enforcement's most powerful weapon. It is certainly its least publicized. The Fourth Amendment to the U.S. Constitution protects all citizens against warrantless searches and seizures. All, that is, except those whose vehicles are impounded.

The Supreme Court of the United States has held that a warrantless search of an impounded motor vehicle does not run afoul of the Fourth Amendment. If the search is conducted according to established police procedures, and not merely as a pretext to avoid the warrant requirement, the high court has held it is perfectly legitimate. An inventory search is necessary when a car is impounded, the court reasoned, to protect the car and its contents, to protect the police against false charges of theft, and to protect the public against the possibility that weapons or contraband might fall into the hands of vandals.

The result of the Supreme Court's analysis is that every impounded vehicle—no matter what the reason for its impoundment—is subject to police inspection from its antennae right down to its floorboards, no warrant necessary.

The officers taking the inventory of Angel's car were not surprised to find it teeming with weapons. Under the seats, they found a sawed-off shotgun, a .25-caliber semiautomatic pistol, and a .38-caliber revolver. In the glove compartment was a set of brass knuckles. And a butcher knife—stained—was removed from the trunk. A laundry list of weapons offenses was added to the charges against Angel. All of the weapons will be sent to the Commonwealth's police laboratory on Tuesday for analysis.

Angel was brought to the District Court holding cells until the magistrate on call could be located to set bail. As a practical matter, though, the officers knew Angel was in for the long haul. Given the nature of the charges against him, the magistrate would be certain to set bail at a figure far beyond anything Angel—or his cohorts—might reach.

It's what the officers found here in the cell block, on Angel's person, that brought about the murder charge. Another .38-caliber revolver, they told Harry, was strapped to the inside of Angel's leg, unloaded. Stuck to the butt of the revolver, they said, was hair, and what looked like human skin and bone fragments.

The revolver, they said, had been used to smash someone's skull. And the knife confiscated from Angel's car easily could have slit a human throat. When Angel refused to account for his whereabouts during the predawn hours of June 14, they booked him for the murder of Jacob Cahoon, Jr.

The image of the cut through Jake Junior's throat is clear in my mind's eye. It was not inflicted with a butcher knife.

Harry says he asked the officers the obvious question: If Angel had murdered Jake Cahoon on June 14, why in God's name would he still have the weapon strapped to his leg on July 4?

The cops just shook their heads. He murdered somebody, they told Harry; that much is certain.

The tape is rewound. Harry and the Kydd and I stare into the wooden file cabinet, watching Angel's arrival at cell six. He is searched, stripped, and held down by four officers while Sergeant Kane cuts the strap from his leg. The Sergeant lifts the revolver with a gloved hand and drops it into an evidence bag. Angel is searched again—all body cavities—before the orange jumpsuit is hurled at him.

All of this is standard procedure. Angel wears an ugly look on his face throughout, but doesn't utter a word. He has been through this before—more than once.

The cell door clangs shut. Angel climbs into the orange jumpsuit and sits on his cot, silent. Nothing happens during the next ten minutes, and I speed up the tape. Not so fast that we can't see what's going on, but fast enough so that we will be able to review four hours of footage in far less than the actual time. Twice, I slow the tape to normal speed when Angel's cell door opens. Both times it is Sergeant Sharkey, with Sergeant Kane right behind him, giving Angel the obligatory repeat opportunities to request an attorney. Angel doesn't say a word to either of them.

By four-fifteen, we've reviewed every minute of activity in cell six since Angel's arrival. And we've seen nothing out of the ordinary. I switch the monitor to channel one, the evidence room, and begin rewinding that camera's footage back to eleven o'clock—more than five hours' worth.

Harry, we've agreed, will go back down to the cell block as often as is possible without arousing suspicion, keeping an eye on the present, as Bobo described it. The Kydd will also keep an eye on the present; he'll check the evidence room every five minutes. I will review the evidence room footage from eleven o'clock forward. As soon as I start rolling the tape, Harry and the Kydd head downstairs.

I allow the tape to run at normal speed while Angel's eleven o'clock arrival spurs an initial flurry of activity on the screen. The first person to appear is Sergeant Sharkey, pushing the Rodriguez crates so far to the left that they can no longer be seen through the camera's lens. He pushes the single Malone crate against them, and it remains visible on the far left side of the screen. The Sergeant hoists up a new crate, empty, and sets it next to Malone. He doesn't bother to label it.

The evidence room grows still for ten minutes or so, and I fast forward through that portion. The camera's clock tells me that Angel is being searched, stripped, and searched again during this time span. When the room grows noisy once more, I slow the tape to normal speed. Sergeants Sharkey and Kane both drop evidence bags into the crate and take turns signing off on a preprinted form on the shelf beside it, presumably accounting for every item they've seized from Angel.

The contents of Angel's car would not have been brought here. All of that will be kept at the station. But anything seized from Angel while in the holding cell should be in that crate. Each item of clothing, separately bagged; the .38-caliber, unloaded revolver; even the strap that held it to his leg. All of it will be sent out on Tuesday for analysis.

The officers switch off the overhead lights in the evidence room and all grows quiet on my screen again. I speed up the tape. Harry returns from the cell block with nothing to report. The guards are annoyed with his small talk, he says, and he doesn't blame them. He'll let them alone for a few minutes.

The Kydd returns just seconds later. The evidence room is still empty, he says, its door still locked. He sits down at my desk—technically, it is still my desk—and jots notes on a legal pad. I am glued to the monitor, running the footage fast now, since nothing is going on in the evidence room. It's almost five o'clock. And I have already reviewed the evidence room footage from eleven to two. I am rapidly reaching the conclusion that we haven't missed a thing. I'm glad, I guess.

Ten minutes later, Harry and the Kydd head back downstairs. The monitor continues to show nothing, and I take the legal pad from my desk to examine the Kydd's notes. He has divided the top sheet into three columns, one for each of the Chatham murder victims. Down the side margin, he has listed basic categories of information, hometown, school, job, number of siblings, date of birth—that sort of thing—and he has started filling in the information for each victim. He is looking for a pattern, but none appears.

I jump up from my stool when I hear a door open. Not a real door, a door on the tape. I stop the tape and rewind just a few seconds. I have to force myself to stare at the monitor, to tear my eyes away from the Kydd's notes. Something about them is unsettling; some visceral reaction makes me want to stare at his notes instead of the monitor.

The camera's clock tells me I am watching the evidence room at two-thirty, two and a half hours ago, a half hour before we got here. I hear the door open, but the lights remain out. Only the inadequate bulbs from the green hallway cast a dim illumination on the scene unfolding.

I watch silently as a lone figure walks directly—in the dark—to Angel's crate. I cannot see the face—the back is toward the camera—but I know who it is, even in the dark. And, during a normal workday, there might well be a legitimate explanation.

But not at two-thirty on Sunday morning.

I am frozen. I watch as the faceless person on the screen takes a wide candle from an interior jacket pocket, strikes a match and lights it, and sets it on the metal shelf, creating a small circle of light in the center of the room. Two gloved hands rummage through the contents of the crate, searching for something specific. The bag holding Angel's .38-caliber revolver is selected, and the gun is removed from the bag with the gloved left hand.

I force myself to breathe normally. There is an explanation for this, I tell myself. The evidence is being handled properly.

A white cloth—presumably sterile—is removed from the right pocket of the suit coat and opened on the shelf, the revolver placed on top. From the left pocket comes a compact plastic box, one that looks like a small sewing kit. It is opened to the right of the gun. An enclosed glass container, the kind we used in high school chemistry class, is removed from the breast pocket and opened to the left of Angel's gun.

I zoom in on the glass container. It is labeled "Cahoon, J." I zoom out again, so I can see it all.

The left gloved hand takes a long pair of tweezers from the plastic box and holds them up in the light of the flame. The tweezers pluck material from the glass jar and plant it on the butt of the revolver, pressing it hard into the other human material already stuck there. I stop the tape, rewind a few seconds, and zoom in on the butt of the gun. I watch the whole procedure again, this time close up.

My hands are planted on the stool in front of me. The room is spinning. I can't swallow. I have to force myself to breathe.

Angelo Santini has just been framed.

CHAPTER 55

▐▐▐

Harry and the Kydd are running after me, calling my name, pleading with me to wait, but I can't. I back the Thunderbird out from behind the courthouse and slam the accelerator to the floor. I grab my cell phone, call the Chatham station house and tell the sergeant in charge everything I can, as fast as I can. The sergeant patches me through to Tommy Fitzpatrick at home and I shout the information all over again. I dial 911 and use what feels like the last of my breath to alert the state dispatcher. Finally, I try Rob Mendell's house. I hear what I knew I would hear—the automated voice of the answering service.

The first hint of daylight is in front of me as I turn east on two wheels out of the county parking lot. A county van—one of the half dozen I parked behind—pulls out immediately after me. The streets are empty. Within minutes, I have the old Thunderbird doing ninety. The county van stays on my tail.

I had barely digested what I saw on the screen when I realized what was missing from the Kydd's notes. He had written the category at the top of the page, next to the "date of birth" column. But he hadn't filled in the numbers yet.

For minutes, it seemed, I could not process my own thoughts. My brain could not grasp what my stomach already knew. Amid all the gruesome patterns we've seen in these Chatham homicides, there is yet another. It is one we all missed, until moments ago, when the Kydd led us to it—almost.

With all of my being I will it to be a mistake, not a pattern at all, just a random string of numbers attached to a random string of murders. But I filled in the blanks myself. I filled in the numbers in the column the Kydd had labeled "date of birth."

Michael Scott was twenty years old when he was murdered.

Skippy Eldridge was nineteen.

Jake Junior was eighteen.

If this is, in fact, a pattern, then the next victim, today's victim, will be seventeen years old.

Two boys lie sleeping at this very moment in Rob Mendell's house. Both just turned seventeen.

And today is the Fourth of July, America's Birthday.

God forgive me. I pray it will be Justin.

CHAPTER 56

All eight Chatham squad cars are at the entrance to Morris Island, at the very end of the causeway, lights blazing and sirens shrieking. A half dozen state cars are here as well. The wooded embankment between Rob's house and Jeff's is peppered with uniforms. The sirens fall silent every few minutes and the Chief shouts through a bullhorn. I can't understand him.

I am headed toward the squad cars as fast as my own car will travel, the county van still on my tail. Somehow, I have to get around them. I have to get to Rob's house. I have to get to Luke and Justin.

A movement to my left catches my eye, though, just as I approach the end of the dike, just before I reach the first of the squad cars. Through the windblown marsh grass, I see activity on the shoreline of the Monomoy Wildlife Refuge. Two people, both inching across the beach at the water's edge. But only one is moving voluntarily; the other is being dragged.

I drive off the road and through a wooden split-rail fence onto the mudflats. I travel as fast as the old car will move, through the marsh, until I see them well enough to know who they are, even through the Chatham fog.

Dr. Jeffrey Skinner. Esteemed pathologist. Serial killer.

And Luke.

I speed straight toward them as far as I can, until the Thunderbird's wheels refuse to turn anymore in the deepening mud. I am out of the car before it stops, my Lady Smith already drawn. I fire immediately. The shot catches Jeff in his left shoulder. It causes only a momentary loosening of his grip on Luke.

I run toward them on someone else's legs. Jeff shifts Luke's weight to his right arm, examines the blood pouring from his own left shoulder for just a few seconds, then turns to his right again, toward Luke.

Luke is motionless.

Someone else's voice screams from my throat. The voice is louder, even, than the ocean wind. "Drop him. Now, Jeff. Drop him or I'll kill you."

I am six feet from them now, both arms outstretched, the Lady Smith aimed at Jeff's head. I slow to a walk. I don't want Jeff Skinner to panic.

Gusts from the Atlantic make walking more difficult when I reach the open beach. "Drop him, Jeff. I swear to God I'll kill you if you don't drop him right now."

Three feet—I am three feet from Jeff Skinner and my son. "Let him go, Jeff. I'll blow your brains out if you don't. God almighty, let him go, please."

I am eighteen inches from them now. Jeff looks directly at me, with eyes that are not his. Planted in the sockets of Jeff Skinner's face are the eyes of someone I've never seen before, someone driven, someone desperate.

I force my eyes away from his frantic stare and steal a glance at his left hand. He's holding a scalpel. It's clean.

The tip of the Lady Smith's barrel is six inches from Jeff's head. I take two more steps—small ones, no big movements. I press the barrel flush against Jeff's left temple and fire.

Jeff's head jerks violently to the right. Fragments of his skull and its contents fly onto the sand behind him. His eyes remain open, staring into mine, and his entire body goes rigid for what seems like a full minute before he releases his grip on Luke. Finally, Jeff Skinner's body falls to the sand.

So does Luke's.

Luke rolls away from Jeff's body, into the incoming tide of the Atlantic. He comes to rest in the shallow water, facedown, and my knees abandon me. I pull myself to him with my hands and elbows; I can't feel my legs. I lift him gently from the water, and roll him over onto my lap. He is not conscious. But he is not cut either. He is breathing. He is alive.

The din of a stampede is behind me. I am afraid to move, afraid to cause further damage to Luke's skull. But my arms don't listen to my fear. They automatically envelop Luke. I press my face against his, begging him to live.

I don't know how much time passes before the paramedics pry my fingers away from my son. Years, maybe.

CHAPTER 57

Late October

Geraldine handled the press afterward. She had known all along about our surveillance in the holding cells and the evidence room. She installed a security camera of her own—in my office. And she monitored the Kydd's every movement.

During the early morning hours of July 4, Geraldine sat in a county van behind the District Courthouse with her own electronic equipment. She watched me while I watched Jeff Skinner manufacture evidence—evidence that would have sent Angelo Santini to Walpole for life just as surely as it did Manuel Rodriguez. And Eddie Malone would have landed there too, eventually, maybe after another stint or two at Bridgewater State Hospital.

It was Geraldine who drove the county van that tailgated my Thunderbird as I sped from the Barnstable District Courthouse toward the Morris Island causeway. The van was never more than a few yards from the Thunderbird, even when I drove through the split-rail fence and onto the mudflats of the Monomoy Wildlife Refuge.

Geraldine had jumped from the county van and drawn her own weapon, I learned later, as soon as the Thunderbird came to a stop. She followed me across the marsh, prepared to take Jeff Skinner down if he lunged at me.

Perhaps I could have spared Luke these long months of suffering if I had worked harder at the practice range, if I had gone more often, as Geraldine said I should. Well-meaning people tell me that the minutes between my first shot and my second didn't matter, that Jeff Skinner had fractured Luke's skull before any of us arrived.

Of course, no one really knows.

CHAPTER 58

The battle of the experts started the day Jeff Skinner's life ended. It continues to this day. Psychiatrists and academicians, many of them Ralph's colleagues, debate the details of Jeff Skinner's mental illness. They begin, of course, with the presumption that he had one. They refine their diagnoses each time a new fact about him is uncovered.

They seem to agree on the big picture. Jeff suffered from post-traumatic stress disorder, they say, stemming from his combat experiences during the Vietnam War. The invitation to speak at Chatham's annual Memorial Day ceremonies just over a year ago is what pushed him over the brink. Preparing his speech, they theorize, is what triggered the flashbacks that made him snap the first time.

They agree on little else.

Some of the experts see significance in the fact that every one of

Jeff's victims was wearing some article of clothing that connected him to the U.S. military. Michael Scott was wearing his U.S. Navy windbreaker; Skippy Eldridge his Otis Air Base cap. Jake Junior was wearing his U.S. Army tee shirt. So was Luke.

But other experts say the victims' clothing had nothing to do with it. The victims were not selected for any particular reason, this group says. These four young men were never targets. They simply happened to be in the wrong places at the wrong times.

Records obtained by the press from the U.S. Marine Corps revealed that Lieutenant Jeffrey Martin Skinner repeatedly complained to his superiors about the youth of the men under his command. The troops were too young, he said over and over again, too inexperienced. Almost every day some of his boys would be brought down by enemy fire. And each new batch of recruits, he complained, was younger than the last.

Some say Jeff's breakdown—and therefore the four Chatham attacks—could have been prevented if proper psychiatric intervention had been available immediately after his return from combat. Others say that the damage done to Jeff's psyche during his years of armed combat was insurmountable. His flashbacks were inevitable, this group says. He was destined to snap.

Still other experts claim that the blame for the four Chatham attacks lies not with Jeff Skinner at all, but with the American public and our national guilt over the Vietnam War. Our failure to deal with that guilt, these experts say, isolates every Vietnam veteran who returned to the States alive. As a nation, we have frozen every one of them in perpetual combat.

Ralph seems to take some comfort from this academic dialogue, as if Luke's ordeal will be made less painful for Ralph to witness if he can understand the forces that drove Jeff Skinner to attack. Ralph actively participates in the debate, writing opinion pieces in scholarly journals, even appearing on television talk shows. He calls me to discuss new theories. He sends me copies of articles.

I don't read them.

CHAPTER 59

Judge Herbert Carroll never returned to the Superior Court bench after the July 4 holiday. First he called Wanda to say he would be taking a much needed vacation. Then he called her back to extend his time off. Finally, he opted for early retirement.

Charlie Cahoon came to the cottage just once, the day after Luke was released from the hospital. He spent a good ten minutes looking closely at Luke asleep on the couch, then took my hands in his and said only, "Oh, Miss Marty." The tears brimming in his sad eyes spilled over then, and he walked out the kitchen door. He hasn't been back. I understand. There is, I know now, a limit to the suffering the human spirit can endure.

Geraldine's campaign is in full swing. The Board of Bar Overseers cleared her of any wrongdoing, agreeing with her that my visit with Eddie Malone and Harry at Bridgewater State Hospital constituted "questionable conduct." Of course, I never testified.

Geraldine's public image did suffer minor damage as a result of the false accusations leveled against Manuel Rodriguez, Eddie Malone, and Angelo Santini. But that damage was more than offset by the dozens of photographs that ran in every newspaper in New England for weeks after Jeff attacked Luke, many of them featuring Geraldine on the Wildlife Refuge, her nine-millimeter Walther PPK drawn, covering me as I approached Jeff Skinner. Those images breathed new life into her "tough on crime" campaign. The polls show her ahead of her male opponent by a healthy margin.

Justin comes over almost every afternoon. He and Luke take Danny Boy for a short walk and then chat with me over a soda or a lemonade at the kitchen table. Rob stops by each day after he leaves the office, visits with us for just a few minutes, and then he and Justin go home together.

I know this arrangement is difficult for Rob. It's hard for him to face Luke and me day after day. He is miserable with guilt about his lack of attention to the Roman numerals, about his unquestioning acceptance of Geraldine's version of reality. But I wasn't sure about the Roman numerals myself until I saw Jake Junior in the morgue. I have told him that more than once.

Luke and I look forward to Justin's daily visits. He pulls us into the present, makes us look to the future, even, to Luke's return to school and, eventually, basketball. Justin doesn't avoid certain topics the way adults do. He makes us laugh out loud by parroting Luke's imitation of Ralph—speaking psychobabble—on the witness stand. He cries freely, as do we, when we talk about the early morning hours of July 4.

It was Justin who filled in the missing details for us; Luke has no memory of that time. The party guests had been picked up at midnight. Luke and Justin sat by the bonfire for another hour, letting it burn down, talking and roasting the last few marshmallows. At one o'clock, they went to bed.

They agreed to a short night's sleep, to go back out to walk the refuge beach and watch the sun come up on Luke's seventeenth birthday. They checked the *Cape Cod Times* and learned that sunrise was expected at five-twelve. Luke set the alarm for five o'clock sharp.

Justin remembers the buzzing of the alarm clock and Luke's shaking him a minute after that. Justin told Luke to forget it and pulled the covers over his head. He remembers feeling kind of bad about it. He remembers Luke's laughing and the sound of the bedroom door closing.

Jeff Skinner never entered Rob Mendell's house that morning. Luke unwittingly went to him.

The Kydd calls each day after he finishes the morning docket. His workload is enormous now that I am gone and Geraldine is campaigning full-time. He tells me he's just holding down the fort until I return. But we both know I'll never go back.

And then there is Harry.

Harry didn't leave my side during the five days Luke spent in the intensive care unit. When Luke's condition was upgraded and he was moved to a regular medical unit, Harry showed up in his room every morning and every evening, before and after work. More than once, I awoke at daybreak in my seat next to Luke's bed to find Harry sound asleep in the chair next to mine. I realized, then, that Harry really does doze off in his suit for a few hours just before going to work. Once again, Geraldine was right.

Now that Luke and I are back in our Windmill Lane cottage, Harry appears on the back deck every morning at sunrise. Even on those rare mornings when I sleep later than that, he is still there, waiting. He brings two large coffees and two cranberry muffins. We sit on the deck while Luke sleeps in, watching the autumn sun climb to its position of prominence over the pounding surf of the Atlantic. Each of us has a coffee; Harry eats both muffins.

At his own request, Harry was relieved of active trial duties as soon as he secured the reversal of the Manuel Rodriguez conviction and the dismissal of the murder-one charges against Eddie Malone and Angelo Santini. Since then, he has spent his days reviewing old case files, looking for other defendants who might have been convicted on the basis of evidence tainted or manufactured by Jeffrey Skinner. I have already told him he won't find any. Michael Scott was Jeffrey's first victim. I saw his number.

Manuel Rodriguez was cleared of the Scott murder and charged with the attempted murder of Jim Buckley in the same proceeding. He entered a not-guilty plea—he's been assigned a new public defender—and will be tried this winter. He never signed a written confession and he denies confessing orally. Harry is prohibited, of course, from testifying against him. But I am not.

The Kydd has already asked me to testify against Rodriguez. I won't do so voluntarily—I won't participate in any criminal prosecution voluntarily—but the Kydd will subpoena me, I am certain. It doesn't really matter. Jim Buckley's positive I.D. will be enough to send Rodriguez back to Walpole. Not for life, but for a decade anyhow.

The Buckley charges are the only ones Manuel Rodriguez will face this winter. I withdrew the assault charges I filed against him. All things considered, I did far more damage to him than he did to me. Technically, the District Attorney's office can pursue those charges without me, of course. But it won't. I told both Geraldine and the Kydd that if they opted to do so, I would testify for the defense. I meant it. And they both knew I meant it.

Angelo Santini pled guilty to three weapons offenses in exchange for the dismissal of the remaining charges against him. He was sentenced to three to five years on each of the firearms convictions and five to seven for the sawed-off shotgun. His sentences will run concurrently and, with time off for good behavior, he will walk away a free man in about two and a half years. He shouldn't, of course. Sergeants Sharkey and Kane were correct when they said he murdered someone. But, so far at least, no body has been found. And as a practical matter, it would be all but impossible to secure a conviction—even with a dead body—after the Commonwealth's employee fouled the evidence.

Judge Richard Gould called a press conference—something no judge in Barnstable County had ever done before—and issued a public apology to Eddie Malone. Eddie walked out of the Barnstable County House of Correction afterward and faced the press with just a little of the old grit back in his eyes, Harry at his side. They both climbed into Harry's Wrangler and the reporters followed it on foot down the driveway until Harry stopped and rolled down his window for Woody Timmons.

"I'm dropping Eddie at the Nor'easter," he said. "You can talk to him there."

Harry expects to finish his file review by November 1, the effective date of his resignation from the Barnstable County Public Defender's office. He plans to take a month off, then open a private criminal defense practice. Private practice, Harry says, will provide a more level playing field, a fighting chance at some semblance of justice. He asked me to join him when I am ready, as a partner. I told him I would think about it. But I haven't.

I am unable to think about any of the things people tell me I should think about. Sometimes, I think long and hard about the criminal justice system—a system I believed in and defended during most of my adult life. I think about Judge Carroll's dynamite charge: ". . . absolute certainty cannot be attained, nor can it be expected . . ." He was wrong. Sometimes, absolute certainty can be attained. Sometimes, it is there to be seen with the naked eye. But the system, choked by its own rules and procedures, does not allow for that.

Judge Carroll is not the only one who was wrong. I was wrong too. I told jurors—hundreds of them, over the years—to use their common sense, to trust their guts, when searching for the truth. I see now that common sense has little to do with it. And most of us, I now believe, could search our souls for the rest of our days without stumbling upon that elusive item called truth.

Other times, I think about Jeff Skinner, a decorated war hero. I think about how difficult it is to recognize evil when it is well dressed and well educated. I think about how easy it is to assign guilt where there is none, how easy it is to leap from accusation to conviction, especially when the accused is rough and unappealing to those of us who are more privileged, those of us who show up for jury duty, those of us who prosecute. I think about how someone as intelligent as Jeff Skinner would understand those facts, could rely upon them.

Most of the time, though, I think about Luke. I sink to my knees each morning and each night and thank God for sparing his young life. I find myself reliving as many moments of that young life as I can. My thoughts are not in chronological order. He is a teenager one minute, rolling his eyes at me, a toddler the next, his little-boy eyes earnest and twinkling. I lose my breath when I reflect on how close we came to the unthinkable.

The tutor has been coming to the cottage for two weeks now. He spends a couple of hours with Luke each morning, and Luke spends an hour or two alone with the books each afternoon. Luke should be ready to return to school in November, the doctors say. With a little extra work, the principal promises, he will graduate with his class.

Luke always dozes off on the couch for a little while around midday, just after the tutor leaves. He still tires easily. Every day during that time I sit perfectly still in the overstuffed chair and watch him while he sleeps. I know he is changed forever. He has come face-to-face with evil, an event that will necessarily alter his view of the world.

I will tell Luke, when he is ready to talk about it, that he shouldn't give up on the world. It's still a worthwhile place. He is still here.

CHAPTER 60

On Sundays, Luke and I take the Thunderbird to People's Cemetery to put fresh flowers on Jake Junior's grave. Daisies or buttercups when we can find them; wild beach roses when we can't. The arrangements we see in florists' shops are too formal, too old. Luke says Jake Junior would laugh at them.

We know, of course, that Jake Junior isn't in that grave. He would never rest there. He would never be at peace so far from his beloved waters of the Atlantic Ocean. Luke says he feels Jake Junior's presence on the beaches of the Monomoy Wildlife Refuge, the very place his own life was spared.

We walk to the refuge every day, usually at dusk. Danny Boy always comes along; he doesn't let Luke out of his sight these days. The three of us sit on the sand at the water's edge and watch the light drain from the sky. Most days, we don't head back to our Windmill Lane cottage until it is dark.

Some days Luke tortures himself with questions about Jake

281

Junior's final moments. Did he realize his assailant was Jeff, someone he knew and liked? Did any words pass between them? Luke is struggling to answer those same questions himself. He just can't remember. And that, I believe, is a blessing.

When darkness falls, we head back to the cottage, Danny Boy leading the way. Some nights, we don't speak at all during our walk. But other nights, Luke asks question after question about the days he cannot remember, the hole in his recent life. Those questions are the easy ones; I'm happy to answer them.

I told Luke how bewildered Danny Boy was while Luke was in the hospital. How he slept in Luke's room every night and looked for him every time the kitchen door opened. How he hung his head and whimpered each time he realized it wasn't Luke coming through the door.

I told Luke about the high school basketball team coming to the intensive care unit during the first days of his hospitalization, even though they knew Luke was unconscious, even though they were allowed to visit with him just once an hour, two at a time, five minutes a pair. The team is practicing now, and Luke and I have gone to the gym a few times to watch. Their hearts are not in it. Their hearts—so young—are heavy.

I told Luke how much Justin missed him and talked to him while he was unconscious. How Justin insisted that Luke's team shirt—number four—be reserved for Luke's return. How Jake Junior's shirt was retired, also at Justin's insistence, and will eventually be hung on the gymnasium wall along with an action photograph of him and a bronze plaque dedicated to his memory.

Some nights Luke asks questions that aren't so easy. Why did Jeff Skinner do what he did? Why didn't he get help after the first one? After the second? How did he live with himself when he was rational, knowing what he had done when he wasn't? How could he have come to Jake Junior's visitation; how could he have sat through Jake Junior's funeral? How did he manage to testify at Manuel Rodriguez's trial? How did he justify—in his own mind—sending others to prison for crimes he committed?

I have nothing to offer in response to these questions. I am always honest with Luke about that. There is simply nothing I can tell him.

There are three things, though, that I tell Luke every night, just before we leave the refuge. "Luke," I tell him, "I'll always help you. And I'll always love you. And those two things will always be true."

Every night he says it back.

ABOUT THE AUTHOR

Rose Connors grew up in Philadelphia, graduated from Mount St. Mary's College, and in 1984 received her law degree from Duke University. A trial attorney for eighteen years, she is admitted to practice in both Washington State and Massachusetts and is a member of the Massachusetts Association of Criminal Defense Lawyers. She lives in the Cape Cod town of Chatham with her husband, Admiralty attorney David Farrell, and their two sons.